GUT SHOT

The words echoed in Gabe's mind. He knew, and it was a terrible knowledge that almost crushed him, that there was nothing he—that anyone—could do for Hears Thunder.

The warrior began to whimper. There were tears in his eyes. His eyes speared Gabe. Asked for help. Asked for the only kind of help that Gabe could give him. Silently asked Gabe to kill him.

Gabe shook his head. He couldn't. He just couldn't.

Hears Thunder moaned again and his eyes continued to plead with Gabe. His mouth worked but he was past forming words.

Gabe raised his rifle.

Hears Thunder did not flinch. He nodded slightly, and waited, an odd expression of peace on his face as Gabe's finger tightened on the trigger.

Gabe fired.

It was over.

He ran on . . .

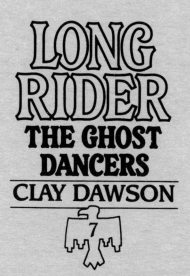

LONG RIDER

THE GHOST DANCERS

CLAY DAWSON

7

CHARTER BOOKS, NEW YORK

THE GHOST DANCERS

A Charter Book/published by arrangement with
the author

PRINTING HISTORY
Charter edition/ November 1989

ISBN: 1-55773-279-5

Charter Books are published by The Berkley Publishing Group,
200 Madison Avenue, New York, New York 10016.
The name "Charter" and the "C" logo are trademarks belonging
to Charter Communications, Inc.

PRINTED IN THE UNITED STATES OF AMERICA

10 9 8 7 6 5 4 3 2 1

CHAPTER ONE

The man rode alone through the mountains as a light snow began to fall and soften the rugged landscape around him. He sat easy in his saddle and the sorrel stallion under him moved with a steady surefootedness through the world that was gradually turning white as the snow continued to fall on this early December day.

The rider occasionally bowed his head slightly as the wind that was roaming through the high country gusted and the falling snow became a briefly stinging on-slaught. Other than that he paid no attention to it or the whining wind.

He looked up but the sun had long since vanished from the sky. Still, he could tell by the quality of the light that night was not far off. He continued riding west, moving downslope now. His body slanted back-ward at an angle to compensate for the sharp dip the ground had suddenly taken. His buckskin-gloved hands rested lightly on his saddle horn, the sorrel's reins lightly wrapped around them.

His name was Gabe Conrad but he was known to the Oglala Sioux among whom he had been raised as Long Rider. The latter name had come from the long ride he had once made as a young boy to carry an important message from one Sioux camp to another along the Powder River, using up two strong horses in the grueling process.

He was slightly taller than six feet and his body was both lean and heavily muscled. His long hair was the color of sand and contrasted sharply with his dark complexion, which was the result of his having spent much of his life in the outdoors where the sun had bronzed his skin and the wind had weathered it. His eyes were gray, the flat color of slate. Deep within them a light seemed to glow, a light that turned bright whenever rage, aroused by men's greed or cruelty, seethed within him.

He wore a heavy buffalo coat which was now covered with a frosting of snowflakes. On the back of the buffalo coat he wore were the painted designs his long dead mother had placed upon it. In its original incarnation, the hide had been a part of the tipi that had sheltered him and his mother during the years they lived among the Lakota people. A blue flannel shirt, worn jeans, battered black boots, and a black slouch hat completed his outfit.

Strapped around his hips and riding high beneath his buffalo coat was a cartridge belt from which hung a holster which housed his .44 caliber Frontier Colt, its butt facing forward for a smooth crossdraw. Sewn to the outside surface of the holster was a sheath containing a sharp knife. In his saddle scabbard was a Winchester rifle which chambered the same .44-40 ammunition his sidearm used.

As he rode on, the snow blurred the outlines of the rocky mountain walls rising around him and coated the equally naked branches of sycamores while nestling among the needles of evergreens. The wind dropped and a stillness filled the land as the snow slowed and then stopped altogether.

Gabe's horse shook its head, sending a shower of snowflakes flying from its mane.

Gabe reached out and patted the sorrel's neck. "Not much farther," he said aloud as he began to stroke his mount's neck. "We'll bed down just as soon as we can find us a suitable place. Somewhere where there's wood and water."

The sorrel nickered and moved on.

The gray light had turned darker by the time Gabe came to the small stream that twisted in and out of a ragged grove of Gambel oaks. He had found the water he had hoped to find. A moment later, as he rode through the grove, he found the wood he had also hoped to find in the form of a rotting deadfall that was decorated with a light covering of snow that looked a little bit like white lace. He moved into the thickest part of the Gambel grove and dismounted.

He stripped his gear from the sorrel and then slapped it lightly on the rump. The animal needed no further urging; it ambled down to the stream, lowered its head, and began to drink.

"Drink as much as you want," Gabe told the horse as he shook out his sweaty saddle blanket and hung it on a low branch of an oak to dry. "You won't be traveling anymore tonight, so drink your fill."

He dropped his saddle, saddle bags, bedroll, and tarp at the thick foot of one of the oaks and then went down to the stream. Kneeling on the ground beside his horse, he took off his gloves and then cupped his hands, using them to scoop up cold water to quench the thirst that had been steadily growing within him until it had nearly matched the ravenous hunger that was causing his gut to mutter noisily.

He rose and began to walk along the stream's bank, his eyes on the ground. He had not gone far when he found the withered remains of some arrowhead plants floating on the water's surface. The plants took their names from the pointed shape of their large leaves which Indians thought resembled the head of an arrow. He stepped into the shallow water and thrust his boot into the stream bed. Within a few moments, he had dislodged several arrowhead roots which he bent down and picked up. He continued harvesting the roots until he decided he had a sufficient quantity. These he carried back to where he had left his gear and placed them on the ground.

Then he went over to the deadfall and kicked it. The dry wood that he dislodged he gathered in his arms and carried back to the spot where he intended to build his fire. But, before starting his fire, he made a sound not unlike a horse's nicker. It brought his sorrel to him. He hobbled the horse for the night among some winter-sparse undergrowth which nevertheless provided good browse.

Then, lighting the wood he had gathered, he blew on the flames until he had a strong fire going. He placed the arrowhead roots he had gathered on the hot coals at the edge of the fire where he left them to roast. He had eaten such roots raw on more than one occasion—usually when he was in a hurry to get somewhere or to get away from somewhere. But now that he had some time, he would enjoy them roasted, a far better way to consume them, he believed, than eating them raw.

He spread his tarp and then his bedroll and sat down on them with his back braced against an oak. He closed his eyes and imagined he could hear the strong heart of the oak behind him beating, beating in the cold winter's night. He heard the sounds his horse was making as it chewed the browse nearby. He almost believed he could feel the earth beneath him throbbing with life—with rich life that was only waiting—waiting for a few more months before it would burst into life and beauty once again.

He felt at peace. He felt one with the Earth, the All Mother to the Sioux; one with the Rock, the Sioux's All Father. He felt as if he could rise and soar on *Tate-tob*, the Four Winds who revealed the god of the Sioux as one yet four: West, North, East, and South, controllers of the weather and the directions. He thought of his early training by a Sioux shaman who taught him to revere *Hunonpa*, the Bear, as the patron of wisdom and medicine, the shaman who also taught him that *Tatanka*, the Buffalo, was the patron of generosity, industry, fecundity, and ceremonies as well as the special overseer of the successful hunter . . .

Tatanka.

Gone now. Almost completely gone now and with *Tatanka*, Gabe feared, were going the People, the Sioux Nation. His sense of peace evaporated. He opened his eyes to the night that had invaded his camp while he was lost in the land of pleasant memories.

But the People, he had heard, had found a new way to save themselves. Not with guns, or bows. Not with another bitter walk upon the warpath against the *wasicu*, the white man. This time salvation would come in the form of a messiah, Gabe had heard, a messiah who would come and save the People who believed in the new Ghost Dance religion which would bring back the buffalo and banish the whites from the world forever.

Despair, Gabe thought. That's what gives life to such last-ditch attempts to reverse the irreversible. From it is born a bitter truth that some believe and some do not. Or cannot. This time it is called the Ghost Dance religion. He wondered if it would work. Or was it just one more road leading to disaster and defeat for the People? He was on his way to find out and he was afraid, deeply afraid, of exactly what it was he would soon find out.

He shook himself as if he were suffering a chill and, in a way, he was—a chill of harsh thoughts. He rose and went to the fire where, using a stick, he raked the arrowhead roots from the embers. They were slightly singed, their skins turned crusty. But he ate them with relish, not waiting for them to cool. Their intense heat nearly burned his tongue and successfully banished his thoughts of the evil fate that the noble *Tatanka* had suffered at the hands of white buffalo hunters. He had thought enough for now on what that evil fate had meant and would continue to mean for the *oyate ikse*, the native people.

When he had finished eating, he went back to his bedroll and sat down upon it. He pulled off his boots and set them to one side, placing his hat upon them. He unbuttoned his buffalo coat and unstrapped his cartridge belt, which he placed next to him and then placed his rifle, which he took from his saddle scabbard, next to it within easy reach. Then he lay down, wrapped himself in his blanket, and surrendered to sleep.

• • •

Two days later, Gabe was crossing a stretch of South Dakota tableland which ended in a rise topped by a stand of white pine. As he rode up and in among the pines, he caught his first glimpse of the Missouri River in the distance ahead of him. Its water glistened in the bright sunlight, reflecting the sun's light as he stared down at it.

He sensed a growing tension beginning to tighten his body as he stared at the town that sat near the eastern bank of the river. Towns meant trouble. He was never comfortable in them, much preferring the free and open world beyond buildings of board and brick, the world that was empty of saloons where whiskey made men mad and unaware of the evil that often stalked the streets and inhabitants of such frontier towns.

But he had to go there. He needed supplies in sufficient quantity to last him for the remainder of his journey. And he also wanted to learn, if he could, what the *wasicu* was saying, if the white man was saying anything at all, about the Ghost Dance religion that was sweeping the reservation like a sudden summer thunderstorm.

He put heels to his horse and rode down from the rise, heading for the town and whatever might await him there, keenly aware of the fact that he was wishing he had already been to the town, done his business, and left it behind him.

He would try, he promised himself, not to attract attention to himself. He would try to behave as any other white man would behave. He would make himself remember that he must look a stranger in the eye when speaking to him or to her and not look away as was considered polite by the Lakota people among whom he had been raised.

It was late afternoon and the sun was going down in an orange blaze of bright glory when he rode into the town. The sun's light harshly illuminated its buildings as well as its residents. The buildings stood out like stark boxes and the people seemed to be on fire, especially their faces. And, most especially, their eyes in their faces that turned toward him as eyes always turned in every town to appraise a stranger riding in among them.

The sunlight revealed questions in those eyes and Gabe heard them as if they had been spoken aloud.

Who is he? Where does he come from? What does he want? Should I fear him? Should I flee from him?

He kept his eyes fixed straight ahead and yet he missed nothing—not the people halting to his left on the boardwalk to watch him ride by and not the man on his right whose nervous hand had come to rest on the butt of his gun.

He drew rein in front of a livery barn and dismounted. He led his sorrel through the open door and into the building's dim interior which reeked of horse sweat, rotting manure, and traces of smoke from a dying farrier's fire.

"Help you?" chirped a rotund little man with a bald head as Gabe approached him.

"I'd like to board my horse overnight. Feed him some good grain. A mix of oats and barley ought to do him fine. Rub him down good and wash out his saddle blanket. He needs a new shoe on his right hind foot. I noticed he'd taken of late to dropping his head every time that foot hits the ground. I checked and found he's thrown a nail and his shoe's gone bad. I'll come by for him in the morning."

"That'll cost you—let's see now." The bald man who

was apparently the stableman began to tick off the items on his fingers while silently adding up the charges. "Four dollars and fifty cents all told," he concluded. "Payable in advance," he added.

Gabe hesitated, somewhat taken aback by the man's way of doing business. "I wouldn't run off and leave a good horse like that," he said, hearing and hating the stony edge to his voice.

"I doubt that you would," said the stableman cheerfully. "But some men have done just that, would you believe it? They come into town, get mixed up with a woman or a marked deck and the next thing you know there's somebody shooting and somebody else dead and I've got a horse on my hands that I might have a hard time selling."

"That sorrel's but three years old. It's big-brisketed as you can see. Got good wind, he has. The gear on him alone's worth a good fifty, sixty dollars."

Before the stableman could say anything more—before *he* could say anything more—Gabe paid in advance for the care of his horse and left the barn.

Cash on the barrelhead, he thought as he emerged into the town that was caught now in the garish grip of the setting sun. *Don't trust anybody.* He shook his head and crossed the street to the hotel.

As he was entering the building, a woman left it. He turned to watch her as she crossed the street and made her way to a building that bore a sign which read: Mother Magee's Home Cooking—Four Bits.

Attractive. Well-built. Walked with a sensuous sway. Hair the color of honey. Her skin—it would, if touched, Gabe was certain, feel as smooth as a calf's ear. Her eyes—what color? He had caught only the briefest of glimpses of her from the front as she passed him so he wasn't sure. He turned and entered the hotel.

At the desk, he asked the clerk behind it for a room for the night. He paid the six bits the clerk asked for and received a key.

"Up those stairs over there, first room on the right," the clerk directed.

Gabe went to the stairs, climbed them, and found the room he had been given for the night. He unlocked the door, then closed it behind him, and lit the lamp that sat on an unsteady table beside the bed.

He took off his coat, tossed it and his hat onto a chair, and then sat down on the bed and pulled off his boots.

He lay down on the bed, his hands clasped behind his head, and imagined he could hear drums, imagined he could hear the pounding of feet as the People danced to bring back the buffalo and danced, too, to bring about the disappearance of the white man.

False dawn's thin gray light crept into Gabe's room the following morning to keep him company while he washed, using the pitcher of water and porcelain basin that sat on top of the room's dresser. The light had not brightened very much by the time he was dressed and out on the street.

Crossing the street, he found that the door of Mother Magee's restaurant was locked. So, he found moments later, was the door of the General Store. But a saloon and the livery barn were open.

He made his way to the stable where he found a boy in attendance instead of the bald man he had met the night before.

"Yes, sir?"

Gabe glanced at the boy. Pale. Thin enough to take a bath in a rifle barrel. In need of some sun and some tempering. Too soft. Skittish-looking.

"That's my horse in that stall over there. I paid the man who was here last night to see to him."

"Yes, sir, I know. Old Elmer, he told me about you."

Gabe arched an eyebrow.

"Said you had long light hair and the gray eyes of a haunt. You've come for your mount, have you?"

"I came to have a look at him." Gabe strode past the wide-eyed boy and entered his horse's stall. He ran his hands lightly over the animal's body, feeling for burrs, for matted hair. He found none. Then he checked his blanket which hung over one of the stall's walls. It had been washed and was dry now. Some barley and oats still remained in the stall's feed bin so it was clear that the stableman had grained the sorrel as ordered.

But, when Gabe methodically began to check the horses's shoes, he found that three of them were in good condition but the shoe on the horse's right hind leg which had lost a nail and been bent out of shape had not been replaced.

"Hey!" Gabe called out to the stable boy as he left his horse's stall.

"Sir?"

"I asked the gent—I recall you said his name was Elmer—to replace my mount's right hind shoe. He didn't do it. Seeing as how I paid to have his shoe fixed, I figure you won't mind if I use your fire and anvil to do the job Elmer should have done last night."

"You're welcome to use whatever you need, sir, but if it's money back you're after, why, you'll have to talk to Elmer. I can't give no refunds. All I can do is tend the stock and sweep up.''

"You can also fetch me a clinch cutter and a pair of shoe tongs," Gabe told the boy.

When he had the tools, he carried them into the stall with him, set them down, and then lifted his sorrel's right hind foot and placed it between his knees. Picking up the clinch cutter, he removed the shoe's nails and then used the shoe tongs to pry the shoe loose. Then he called out to the stableboy to heat up the forge.

When the fire was hot enough to suit him, Gabe selected a shoe from among the many hanging on nails on the barn wall and, using tongs, heated it. When it was cherry-red, he withdrew it and holding it against the anvil, he proceeded to hammer the new shoe into a shape that would fit his horse's hoof.

When he was satisfied with what he had done, he plunged the new shoe into a barrel of water that stood near the forge to cool it and then proceeded to nail it in place on the sorrel's hoof.

"I've got some breakfast to get and some supplies to buy," he told the stableboy. "Then I'll be back to take my horse off your hands."

He left the barn and joined the crowd that had gathered in front of Mother Magee's restaurant since his last visit.

"What time does this place open?" he asked a man standing beside him.

"Seven sharp," was the answer.

"The food's worth waiting for, is it?"

"Best you can buy this side of the Missouri."

When the restaurant opened several minutes later, Gabe joined the rush of men and women for a table inside. He was one of the lucky ones; he got a table.

Those who were not quick enough stood waiting by the door for their turn to sit down at a table and buy breakfast.

When a waiter appeared at his table, Gabe ordered a beefsteak, pan bread, and scrambled eggs.

"Coffee, sir?" inquired the waiter. "Tea?"

"Milk'll be fine."

Later, when the waiter had reappeared with his breakfast, Gabe was just about to cut into his bloody beefsteak when he noticed her among the throng of people near the door. She was the woman with the sensuous walk whom he had seen the night before as he was entering the hotel and she was leaving it. He immediately rose and went over to where she was standing.

Reminding himself to look her in the eye—her eyes were emerald he noted—the way any other white man would do, he said, "Ma'am, I know you must be hungry so I've taken it upon myself to invite you to share my table instead of you having to stand here and wait for who knows how long before you get your turn at an empty table."

"It's most kind of you to offer to share your table with me," she said. "I shall be pleased to do so."

He turned and made his way back to his table, the woman following him. He sat down moments before she did. She had, he thought vaguely, seemed to have been waiting for something. What? He had no idea. He beckoned to the waiter.

When the man arrived at the table, he said, "The lady here's hungry."

"I'll have a soft-boiled egg, please, and a cup of tea."

When the waiter had gone, the woman spoke to Gabe. "My name is Lorelei Adams."

"Pleased to make your acquaintance, Miss Adams. My name's Conrad. Gabe Conrad."

"Well," Lorelei said somewhat nervously. "This place is really quite popular judging by the crowds it draws. Do you come here often?"

"This here's my first time."

"Then I take it you don't live in town."

"I don't."

"You're just passing through?"

"Heading west, yes, ma'am."

"I, too, am just passing through town. I'm from Boston and am on my way to the Standing Rock Indian Reservation. I shall be teaching at the Indian boarding school there. Mr. McLaughlin at the agency is sending someone to meet me at the hotel this morning."

The waiter appeared and placed a cup containing the egg Lorelei had ordered in front of her and then poured her a cup of tea.

Gabe cut a piece of meat from his beefsteak and forked it into his mouth. He followed it with a forkful of scrambled eggs and a piece of pan bread.

As he continued eating, he watched Lorelei delicately remove the top of her egg's shell and just as delicately begin to spoon the shell's contents into her mouth.

When she saw him watching her, she blushed.

"I hope I don't make you nervous."

"You don't, Mr. Conrad. It's just that I'm not accustomed to the company of cowboys."

"I'm no cowboy."

"Oh, I thought—your dark complexion, the buffalo

coat you're wearing—I'm sorry. I just assumed you were a cowboy who lived the outdoor life.''

"You heard about what's been happening on the reservation?'' he asked, ignoring her remarks.

"I'm not sure what you mean.''

"I'm talking about the Ghost Dance religion that's got the Indians all excited.''

"Oh, yes, I have heard something about that.''

"What have you heard?''

"Well, people here in town have been talking about it and seem rather uneasy about it. Upset, I suppose you might say. They fear an Indian outbreak. Do you think there will be one, Mr. Conrad?''

Gabe noted the fear in Lorelei's eyes as she asked her question. He also noted the way she was now nervously twisting her spoon instead of using it to consume the remains of her egg.

"If you're afraid the Sioux might rise, maybe you oughtn't to go on to the reservation.''

Lorelei blanched and then, with an effort, squared her shoulders and said, "I have a moral obligation to fulfill my commitment to Agent McLaughlin. We have a duly executed contract concerning my job, my duties, my salary—and I don't want to let him down, not now that I've come this far. Mr. McLaughlin has been eminently fair with me and I want to be fair with him.''

"What's your opinion of this McLaughlin fellow?''

"I haven't met him personally, you understand. But I must say his letters sounded very gracious and straightforward. I'm looking forward to working with him at the agency. Do you know the man?''

"No. But I've heard it said that he's brave and resourceful and, most important, fair where it comes to dealing with the People.''

"The People? I'm afraid I don't follow you."

Gabe hesitated. He should have said that McLaughlin was fair in his dealings with the Indians, not the People. But—well, why not tell the lady the truth?

"I spent my boyhood among the Sioux who call themselves the *oyate ikse*, the native people," he explained.

He had half-expected Lorelei to recoil at his announcement. She didn't. On the contrary, she looked at him with renewed interest and even leaned across the table toward him as she said, "That explains it."

"Explains what?"

"I don't mean to be rude, Mr. Conrad. But I couldn't help noticing that you didn't escort me to your table. Instead, you simply let me follow you here. When we reached the table, you didn't seat me as most gentlemen would have done. I suppose the niceties of the white world are not altogether familiar to—to a man with your unusual background."

"You're mostly right on that score, Miss Adams. I'll confess to you though that what you call the niceties of the white world sometimes strike me as just plain foolishness."

Lorelei's hand flew up to cover her mouth as she was seized by a brief fit of giggling. Then, sobering, she confided, "I feel exactly the same way. Especially concerning the way gentlemen are expected to behave toward ladies. Why, they are forced to act as if we are all helpless ninnies unable to open a door for ourselves or to step down unaided from a carriage. Such behavior can be a trial to any woman with a mind and spirit of her own."

"I knew you for a woman with her own mind and

spirit the minute I laid eyes on you.'' Gabe gave Lorelei a mischievous smile.

"You must promise me faithfully not to reveal my secret.''

"I promise you, Miss Adams. Your secret's safe with me. I just hope you can trust my word despite my wild Indian upbringing.''

"Was it truly so wild?''

"You could say that, yes, you most certainly could.''

"How interesting. I wish I had more time to spend with you. I'd love to hear about your boyhood. It would be a perfectly splendid opportunity for me to learn more about the children I am going to teach when I reach the agency. And I must say, Mr. Conrad, I am grateful for your assurances concerning the character of Agent McLaughlin. Based on what you have told me about him, I'm sure the two of us will get along just fine.''

"From all I've heard, McLaughlin stands head and shoulders above most Indian agents. He really knows how to run a reservation and what's more he cares about the People. Not like most agents. Certainly not like Agent Royer down at Pine Ridge.''

"I'm not familiar with the name.''

"The Sioux on that reservation are. Do you know what they call Royer, who I've heard lacks good judgment, courage, and a whole host of other qualities a man in his position needs to run a reservation?''

Lorelei leaned even closer to Gabe, so close that he could smell the scent of rosewater she was wearing which he found arousing. "The People call Agent Royer *Lakota Kokipa-Koshkala*. That's Sioux for Young-man-afraid-of-Indians.''

This time Lorelei didn't giggle. This time she burst

out into loud laughter. Then, quickly recovering, she busied herself with the remains of her egg and tea.

When both were gone, she looked up at Gabe and said, "It's been a pleasure meeting you, Mr. Conrad. I must be going now so that I don't miss whomever Mr. McLaughlin is sending to pick me up. If you'll excuse me."

This time, as Lorelei rose, so did Gabe, remembering his white man's manners.

"I wish you a safe journey, Miss Adams," he said. "Don't you bother paying for what you ate. I invited you to join me so I'll take care of the bill."

Lorelei nodded, smiled, and a moment later was gone.

Gabe drank the last of his milk and then paid for his and Lorelei's meals. Upon leaving the restaurant, he headed for the general store where he bought four cans of tomatoes, some sowbelly, and two pounds of dried apples. He asked the storekeeper for a flour sack to pack his supplies in and then left the store, intending to pick up his horse and ride out.

But he halted just outside the store at the sight of three men gathered in front of the saloon, two of them, both white, with guns in their hands. Those two were harassing the third man, an Indian, whose back was to Gabe.

One of the pair pushed him. The other man tried to trip him and then raised his gun, aimed it directly at the Indian facing him and said, loud enough for the crowd that was gathering to hear. "So let's see how you do that damned Ghost Dance of yours!"

The man just addressed shook his head. He thrust his hands into the pockets of the sack coat he was wearing and planted his legs, which were clad in woolen trousers, far apart as if to steady himself.

One of the other two men reached out and knocked his low-crowned black hat off.

As the man bent to retrieve his hat, one of the other men brought his knee up to crack sharply against the hatless man's chin. The blow straightened the bent-over man, turned him, and sent him staggering several steps toward Gabe.

Their eyes met.

Gabe noted the blue dot tattooed on the forehead of the young man he now was able to recognize as a Sioux Indian.

One of the pair of men reached out, seized the Sioux by the shoulder, and spun him around. "You do your little dance for us or we'll turn you into dead meat, Injun."

Gabe dropped his sackful of supplies and strode purposefully toward the men.

CHAPTER TWO

When he reached them, he took up a position at the side of the unarmed Sioux with the tattoo on his forehead who was, Gabe estimated, between twenty and twenty-five years of age. "What seems to be the problem here, gents?" he asked the other two men in a low tone.

"Ain't no problem, mister," one of the men told him. "We're just trying to get this here Injun to do his dance for us."

"His Ghost Dance," added the second man. "We want to watch him make us white folk disappear from the face of the earth."

Guffaws from some of the men in the crowd.

Giggles from a few of the watching women.

"These Injuns," said the first man who had spoken, "they got themselves a notion that they can dance back the buffalo or some such fool thing and also rid the world of the whites at the same damn time. Well, we just want to give this Injun a chance to do his stuff only it turns out he's a bullheaded type of fellow. He won't dance.''

"But we figure we can make him," declared the man's companion confidently. "You want to watch, you're welcome."

Gabe said nothing. He stood there, his body taut, all his senses alert. Waiting. Watching.

One of the two men shouted, "Dance, Chief!"

His companion fired a shot that slammed into the dirt at the Sioux's feet.

It made him jump to one side.

The second shot from the same gun made him jump in the opposite direction.

A swift series of shots followed, forcing the Sioux to leap from side to side, to jump backward, to spring forward to avoid being shot in the foot.

Someone in the crowd began to play a tune on a Jew's harp. Someone else began to clap. Soon others were also clapping.

The man who had fired the volley of shots was in the process of reloading his revolver when Gabe said, in a voice loud enough to be heard above the music of the Jew's harp and the crowd's rhythmic clapping, "Leave this man alone."

"Man!" hooted one of the two men facing the Sioux. "Listen to him, Baxter. He just called this mangy Injun a man."

"Well, Royce, what do you expect from a man that's crazy—and he surely is? You can tell by the loco look in those spooky gray eyes of his."

"Crazy as a cow at heel fly time," agreed Royce. Then, to Gabe, "Step aside, mister. Baxter and me don't hurt crazies or cripples."

The crowd stopped clapping. The Jew's harp fell silent.

To the young man beside him, Gabe said, "Let's go."

"Mister," Baxter snarled, "why don't you try minding your own business?"

"I'm making this my business," Gabe replied calmly.

"How come you're taking the side of the Injun?" a genuinely puzzled Royce asked, his tone querulous. "You're as white as we are and he's nothing but a heathen savage, never mind those clothes he's wearing to try to look like a white man."

Gabe turned and began to walk away, his body tense, his mind speculating on whether or not it was a good idea to turn his back on Baxter and Royce. He became aware that the Sioux was not following him even before he heard the first shot sound behind him. He spun around to find the Sioux hopping about to avoid being struck in the foot by one of Baxter's bullets. The man presented a pathetic picture, one not of merriment but of humiliation.

"Hold your fire!" Gabe ordered Baxter at the top of his voice.

The firing intensified, taken up by Royce in a gesture of defiance. Both men, as they fired, glanced at Gabe, grinning.

"Hold your fire," Gabe repeated as loudly as he had spoken the first time, "or I'll see to it that you hold it."

"How?" Baxter shouted with glee. "Without a gun you can't—"

"I've got a gun and I can," Gabe shot back.

"But can you shoot it with that bad-bent trigger finger of yours?'' Royce taunted. "Hell, the only thing you're good for, mister, is telling tall tales, not shooting at people.''

Gabe's left hand flashed across his body to bury itself momentarily beneath his buffalo coat. Then it emerged holding his Frontier Colt. He leveled the weapon at Royce, then shifted it slightly so that it pointed at Baxter. He said nothing.

Neither did anyone else for a long tense moment.

Then Baxter spoke, his eyes flicking from the gun in Gabe's hand to Gabe's impassive face. "By God, the bastard *has* got himself a gun."

Royce chuckled. "He thinks his one iron is equal to the two of ours. Damn fool, that man."

"Come on," Gabe said to the Sioux and began backing away from the confrontation.

Baxter and Royce watched him. So did the men and women in the crowd.

The standoff continued as Gabe backed toward the livery stable. On the way to it, he paused and retrieved the flour sack that contained the provisions he had bought. Then he continued his journey without breaking stride.

When he was only yards away from the livery barn's door, he spoke to the man by his side. The man left him and ran into the barn. Moments later, he emerged leading Gabe's sorrel. Gabe took the horse's reins in his free hand and stepped into the saddle. He spoke again and the man he had rescued promptly leaped up behind him.

Gabe caught a glimpse of Lorelei Adams standing with a valise by her feet under the overhang in front of the hotel.

Then he turned his horse and slammed his heels into

its ribs. As he went galloping down the street, a shot rang out behind him. He heard it whine uncomfortably close to his right ear. He turned in the saddle, leaned out around the man behind him, and returned the fire— a single shot which went where it had been aimed— into the dirt directly in front of Royce's boots.

"Next time, I'll aim higher!" he shouted at Royce.

When the warning had no effect on Royce, who fired again, Gabe made good on his promise. His second shot blasted into Royce's calf, toppling the man to the ground.

"I'll shoot still higher next time," Gabe shouted and was gratified when neither Royce nor Baxter fired again. He galloped out of town toward the river beyond it.

When they reached the river, both men dismounted and Gabe asked, "What were you doing in that town?"

"I lived there," answered his companion. "In a shed behind the saloon where I worked."

"How come those clothes?" Gabe indicated the man's sack coat, woolen trousers, and townsman's shoes.

"In the white world it is not good to look like an Indian."

Gabe nodded. A good answer. Maybe even a wise one, especially for a man so young. "If you go back there—those men, they're not likely to leave you be, you know."

"I know. So I will not go back. Maybe I will go to some other town."

"How come you want to live and work in a town in the first place? Most white towns don't exactly welcome Indians with open arms."

"That is true. But on the reservation, we go hungry. Some months, little beef ration. Some months, no beef ration. My sister is hungry. Her daughter is hungry. So I go to do white man's work to get white man's money to buy food to take to them in the tipi we share.''

''Agent McLaughlin, how does he feel about that?''

''I do not tell him so he does not know what I do.'' A pause, and then, ''I have a question to ask you.''

''Shoot.''

''How is it that you, a white man, go against your own kind to help me?''

''Those people back there, they're not exactly my kind.''

The young man frowned, obviously puzzled.

''Well, in a way they are my people, I reckon. At least insofar as my skin's white, though you'd hardly know it the way the sun's turned me about as brown as a berry. But I know that's not answering your question. Let me put it to you this way. I didn't want those gunmen back in town to kill you even though I knew—'' Gabe, smiling, pointed to the blue dot tattooed on the young man's forehead, ''—that the mark you've got would keep *Hihan Kara*, the Owl Maker, from pushing you off the Ghost Trail once you were dead and gone.''

When his companion's frown deepened, Gabe said, ''You're wondering how I know about *Hihan Kara*.''

''I am.''

''I grew up with the Oglala Sioux. Didn't leave them until I was fourteen, though I'm not all that sure I ever really did leave them except in a physical sense.''

The young man's frown was replaced by a broad smile. He pointed a finger at Gabe and said two words: ''Long Rider.''

It was Gabe's turn to smile. ''That's what they called me.''

''I have heard talk of you around many campfires.

The People say you rode many miles with a message that had been entrusted to you when you were fourteen. They say two horses died under you during your long ride. They speak and sing of you even to this day. They tell of Long Rider with the yellow hair and eyes the color of smoke who saved an entire village full of people from the white man's guns because he would not stop when weary so that he might deliver the important message he carried.''

"The Lakota give me too much credit," Gabe said modestly.

"The People, as you must know, do not give credit where credit is not due."

Gabe remained silent.

"I thank you for what you did for me today in town. Now I will go back to the reservation."

"Which one?"

"Standing Rock. My name—Hears Thunder. I have a lodge in Sitting Bull's camp on the Grand River."

"That's northwest of here," Gabe mused.

"You go that way, Long Rider?"

"Well, I was more or less planning on heading due west to the Cheyenne River Reservation or maybe southwest to the Pine Ridge Reservation."

An image of the lovely Lorelei Adams, who had said she would be teaching school at the Standing Rock Reservation, blazed momentarily in Gabe's mind. It decided him. "Let's get back aboard my horse," he said to Hears Thunder. "I'll take you to Sitting Bull's camp."

Later that day Gabe and Hears Thunder, when they reached the Grand River, stopped and made camp for the night.

Hears Thunder built a fire while Gabe unpacked his sackful of supplies. As evening darkened into night, both men sat beside the fire, holding chunks of sowbelly they had speared on sticks over the flames. Fat fell from the meat to sizzle and spit in the fire.

Gabe handed one of the two cans of tomatoes he had opened with his knife to Hears Thunder and, when the meat was browned and crisped, they both ate hungrily, saying nothing until the food had been completely devoured.

Then Gabe, hunkered down before the fire, said, "I've heard about the Ghost Dance religion that folks say has got the People all stirred up. What can you tell me about it, Hears Thunder?"

"Some of us, we dance. Others say it is only foolishness. Sitting Bull has danced but he has also said— I heard him so say with my own two ears—that nothing can bring a dead man back to life, which is one of the things believers in the religion think will happen if they dance."

"The dead will become the quick again, you mean?"

Hears Thunder nodded. "Dancers, some of them, have visions—they travel to the spirit world. There they meet those who have walked the Ghost Trail in the sky. It makes them happy to visit with the ones they loved who have died."

Gabe thought of his dead wife. "I heard the People believe the religion will somehow or other bring back the buffalo—and make the white man disappear." His last words sent a chill coursing through him.

Hears Thunder seemed to have guessed what he was thinking. "I do not believe you will be harmed, Long Rider, when the day comes for the white man to vanish. You are of the People, not really a white man."

"What about you? Do you believe?"

Hears Thunder cocked his head to one side. He spread his hands, palms up, in front of him. He shrugged. "I do—and I do not. It is a mystery more difficult to understand than the mystery of the Great Spirit, *Wakan Tanka*. He paused a moment before adding in a wistful tone of voice, "I *want* to believe. I want very much to believe."

"It would be a good thing," Gabe said thoughtfully, "if the old days would come again. If the buffalo would once again cover the land like a big blanket. If the *wasicu* would disappear and the People could be once again free of them and their ways."

"But you do not believe this will happen." A statement, not a question.

"I guess you could say I've got an open mind where the Ghost Dance religion is concerned," Gabe said, knowing he was evading the issue. "I need to know more about it before I make up my mind."

"Chief Kicking Bear believes," Hears Thunder declared. "So does Chief Big Foot. Both of them have held Ghost Dances on the Cheyenne River Reservation."

"I hear all the Indian agents have been trying to stop the dancing."

"They have. They have sent word to the land where the sun rises. Because of that soldiers come to reservations. Many soldiers. Foot soldiers and pony soldiers, they both come. They are everywhere now. Whites fear the Ghost Dance will lead to rebellion. They think we will put on the paint and walk on the warpath against them." Hears Thunder gave Gabe a sidelong glance and said, "They think we will dance ourselves crazy and come after them with lance and tomahawk."

Had there been a twinkle in Hears Thunder's eye? Gabe wasn't sure. Perhaps it had just been the reflected light of the leaping flames.

"That is why the soldiers come," Hears Thunder continued. "White men fear the Ghost Dance and what it means to the People. What the white men fear, they hate. What they hate, they kill."

Gabe offered Hears Thunder some dried apples. For the next few minutes, the two men ate the fruit in silence. Then Gabe broke the silence with, "I thought the People had made themselves some kind of clothes—or so I heard, at any rate—that were supposed to stop bullets so they couldn't be killed while wearing whatever it is they'd made for themselves."

"They—we—call it the Ghost Shirt. We paint it with symbols from our dreams. Yes, it is said no white man's bullet can pass through it." Hears Thunder spat out some apple seeds.

"Do you believe that?"

"I do not say if I do or do not believe it." He spat out still more apple seeds. "If it be true, I have to ask myself a question."

Gabe waited while Hears Thunder picked his teeth with a twig.

"If it be true that the Ghost Shirt will not let bullets pass through it, I ask myself why then do the People not also make for themselves Ghost Leggings, Ghost Moccasins, Ghost Hoods with holes for eyes and nose to put over the head."

Gabe suppressed a smile, a bitter smile. The fellow's a cynic, he thought. Hears Thunder has himself a mind and that can be a burden for a man, though it also has its uses. Or maybe, he thought, the man's not a cynic at all. Maybe all he is is a down-to-earth realist.

"With ghost leggings and other ghost clothing, no wounds in legs, feet—not anywhere," Hears Thunder declared, breaking Gabe's reverie.

Had his eyes twinkled when he spoke? Again, Gabe wasn't sure.

"Wovoka," Hears Thunder said, looking off into the dark distance beyond the light of the fire.

"Beg pardon?"

"Wovoka," Hears Thunder repeated. "That is the name of the man who began it all."

"You mean the Ghost Dance religion?"

Hears Thunder nodded. "Wovoka is a Paiute. One day he has a revelation. In a trance, he is told that the dead will rise and live again. The buffalo will return in numbers too many for ten men to count in two moons. The white men will disappear. Wovoka taught his people the dance that he learned in the spirit world.

"Kicking Bear brought the new religion to the Lakota after Kicking Bear went all the way to Nevada to meet Wovoka. It is the Lakota who add the ghost shirts to the religion. It is the ghost shirts that make the white men afraid. The white men, they think why do Indians need ghost shirts to keep them from harm unless they plan to rise up and strike us all down.

"Such talk is foolishness. Even Agent McLaughlin at Standing Rock agency has said so. Those two men in town—the men with guns that shot at my feet. They fear the Ghost Dance religion. That is why they treat me as they did. They mask their fear with the bad joke they play on me."

"That bad joke, as you call it, could have wound up with you dead if they'd taken it far enough," Gabe commented pointedly.

"Yes, that is so." Hears Thunder paused a moment

before continuing. "Agent McLaughlin thinks Sitting Bull is the leader of the Ghost Dance among the People at Standing Rock. Agent McLaughlin thinks Sitting Bull uses the Ghost Dance to make himself once more the leader of the People."

"Is that true?"

"I do not think so. I told you before that Sitting Bull does not believe the dead can return to us. Now our talk has made a circle. We come back to where we started. I sleep now."

Gabe, as Hears Thunder made himself ready for the night on the leeward side of a dense growth of chokecherry bushes, rose and went to his horse. He stripped his gear from it and then led it to an area away from the camp where the graze was, if not excellent, at least good. There he left the animal standing with its rump to the wind and returned to the fire. He spread his tarp and then his saddle blanket on the ground near it, placed his sidearm on the ground beside him, and then wrapped himself in his blanket.

He lay there staring up at the icy stars for a few minutes but then sleep claimed him and brought him a dream that was loud with what he at first thought were cannons booming. But then he realized that what he was hearing was the sound of thousands of buffalo racing across the plains, their hooves loudly pounding the ground, the dust they raised in passing almost blotting out the rising sun behind them. It seemed, in Gabe's dream, as if the sun itself had given birth to the buffalo. It seemed as if it was from the sun's fiery womb that the animals raced again into the world from which they had been driven by white men with deadly .50 caliber Sharps rifles in their hands.

• • •

Gabe awoke but did not open his eyes. Nor did he move so much as a muscle. He lay wrapped in his blanket, listening, sensing the still-dark world around him. He was not sure what had awakened him. Perhaps he had heard a sound in his sleep. Perhaps it had been the cry of a nightbird. He didn't know what it was that had awakened him, he knew only that something had. He opened his eyes.

Darkness. The stars still glittering coldly above him. In the east, the first gray glow of false dawn.

He heard nothing. Saw nothing. As he continued listening carefully, his hand crept toward his revolver and then closed on its butt. His finger slid through the guard and came to rest on the gun's cold trigger.

He remained where he was, lying motionless, only his eyes moving.

Gradually, as the gray light in the eastern sky grew brighter, he relaxed. He heard a fox cough not far away. Maybe that was what had awakened him. A fox making its nocturnal sounds in search of food or a female.

He threw off his blanket, sat up, holstered his gun, stretched, yawned.

By the time Hears Thunder had awakened and made his way into the woods to relieve himself, Gabe had a fire going and some sowbelly roasting on the ends of sticks stuck in the ground and slanted over the flames.

The sun, though not yet above the horizon, was reddening the clouds floating in the eastern sky when Gabe turned to gaze southward.

Hears Thunder gazed at him. "You hear something?"

Gabe bent down and placed his right ear against the ground. Then, straightening, he said, "Horses. Coming this way."

"Some of the People," Hears Thunder speculated.

Gabe shook his head. "The horses I heard were shod."

"Pony soldiers," Hears Thunder said and Gabe thought he saw fear flare in the man's eyes.

Moments later, they came riding into the small camp. A cavalry troop and a Crow Indian scout.

As the men drew rein, one of the troopers said, addressing the scout by his side, "You said there were two Indians, Horse Chaser. But one of these men is white."

Gabe stared at the Crow scout, distaste twisting his features. *The Crow, ancient enemy of the Lakota,* he thought. *That one there must be who I heard during the night, sneaking around to see what he could see, and he saw me and Hears Thunder.*

"May I ask what you two are doing here?" the trooper asked, his gaze shifting from Hears Thunder to Gabe.

"We might just as easy ask you the same question," Gabe responded.

The trooper's eyes narrowed. "You might," he said coldly. "Before you do, I'll tell you. I'm Corporal Everson. I am from Troop B of the Seventh Cavalry under the command of General Forsyth as are the men with me. We are stationed at the Pine Ridge reservation south of here along with seven other troops, to help keep the peace."

"I didn't know there was a war," Gabe commented mildly.

His remark caused Everson's upper lip to twitch.

"We are out here on the plains," Everson continued, "to round up a number of Indians who left the reservation and headed for the Badlands northwest of the White River in South Dakota. We—''

"You've gone a pretty far piece out of your way, soldier," Gabe pointed out. "You're on the Standing Rock reservation now."

"I know that very well and am therefore in no need of you to tell me so. But we have been in hot pursuit of the Indians I mentioned since they broke and scattered in every direction imaginable. Horse Chaser here, our scout, picked up your trail just before dawn this morning and reported your presence here. May I ask what you are doing in the area?''

"A little of this, a little of that," Gabe answered, enjoying the anger he saw blazing in Corporal Everson's eyes at his deliberately evasive manner.

Through clenched teeth, Everson said, "May I request that you be a bit more specific, if it's not too much trouble."

"No trouble at all. We've been doing a little hunting, a little fishing, me and my friend here, whose name is Hears Thunder. My name's Gabe Conrad.''

"You seem to have had no luck," Everson observed.

"Lakota," Horse Chaser interjected, pointing at Hears Thunder. "Bad Indian."

"Bad hunter too," Gabe said with forced cheer. "Hasn't caught so much as a rabbit in his snares."

"Where are you heading?" Everson asked.

"To the camp of Sitting Bull on Grand River," Hears Thunder answered, speaking for the first time.

"And you?" Everson prompted, glancing at Gabe.

"Same place."

"What business have you there?" Everson persisted.

"None that need concern you."

"Everything that happens these days here in Sioux

country,'' Everson stated, ''is the business of the army. We have men deployed on all four reservations in this area as ordered by Colonel Nelson A. Miles. There are troops from Fort Robinson in Nebraska on the Pine Ridge reservation and there is also a battalion of the colored Ninth Cavalry there under the command of Major Henry. Captain Capron commands a battalion of the Fifth Artillery, Colonel Wheaton commands a company of the Eighth Infantry, and eight companies of the Eighth are under the command of Colonel Wheaton.''

''You fellows must be expecting Armageddon from the sound of things.''

''It is time we showed ourselves in force to keep the Indians from their infernal Ghost Dance ceremonies that are stirring up so much trouble. At Rosebud reservation we've got two troops of the Ninth Cavalry and along the south fork of the Cheyenne River Lieutenant Colonel Offley has taken a position with seven companies of the Seventeenth Infantry. East of him—''

Gabe held up a hand. ''You got anybody left to defend the rest of the country?''

''I must say you are insultingly sarcastic, sir.'' Then Everson added, ''If you're heading, as you claim to be, for Sitting Bull's camp, I'd suggest you would do well to be on your way.''

As Everson rode out with the other three troopers, Horse Chaser said, ''Sitting Bull, him one bad Indian.''

''*Him* one bad Indian,'' Hears Thunder muttered under his breath but loud enough for Gabe to hear as the men rode away. ''Bad like all Crows,'' he added. ''They hate the Lakota; we hate them.''

''Since when's the army been using Crow Indians for scouts?''

''Long time now. They are part of Lieutenant Robinson's company of scouts. They like to work for army against Lakota. Pay is good and it is a way for them to do harm to their old enemies—to us.''

''We'd best be getting along,'' Gabe said and went for his horse.

Later, when he had the animal ready to ride, he lingered only long enough to stamp out the campfire. Then both men boarded the sorrel and rode out, following the Grand River as it wound its way westward.

They had not gone far when, as they topped a rise, Gabe drew rein and sat his saddle, staring down at Corporal Everson and the other pony soldiers as they herded a band of Sioux southward toward Pine Ridge.

''They look a sorry lot,'' Gabe said, his voice tinged with sadness as he watched the Indians, all of them on foot, trudge across the plain under the cool December sun.

''With so many soldiers about, the People are much afraid,'' said Hears Thunder as he, too, watched the ragged procession of men, women, and children make their slow way south under the eyes of the troopers.

''That's why they jumped the reservation and headed for the Badlands?''

''Yes. They think to hide there until soldiers go away and they are no longer in danger.''

''Are they in danger?'' Gabe asked, shielding his eyes with a hand to block out the sun as he watched the riders herding their charges along like so many cattle.

''They fear the soldiers,'' Hears Thunder answered. ''Who can say if they are right to do so. There is hot talk in the white settlements along the river.

''I told you the whites think the People will come dancing after them to take their scalps—and their lives.

So the soldiers come to save the whites from us. Always before when the soldiers come, Death came riding with them."

"You think there will be shooting?"

"Maybe so. Already the soldiers have broken up some of the Ghost Dances. One day maybe someone will resist—maybe many will. Then the bullets will fly and men will die. Death songs will be sung for the wind to hear. Colonel Drum and his pony soldiers then will sing their songs of victory over the corpses of the People."

"Who's this Colonel Drum?"

"He is commander of the pony soldiers at Fort Yates which is forty miles from Standing Rock agency."

As Hears Thunder spoke, the sun had disappeared in a darkening sky. As he and Gabe rode down from the rise, snow began to fall. Within minutes, it had swallowed the Sioux and the soldiers as if they had never existed.

CHAPTER THREE

It was late afternoon when they arrived at Sitting Bull's camp on the Grand River.

As they approached it, Hears Thunder slid down from Gabe's horse and, walking a few paces ahead, led the way in among the tipis clustered along the bank of the river.

Gabe, as he followed Hears Thunder on his sorrel, had an eerie feeling, one he could not put a name to. He felt, in an odd way, as if he were coming home. It was a warm feeling, a friendly feeling, one he wished he would never lose but one which he knew was basically false. He was not coming home. He had no home. All he was doing was returning as a man to the sights and sounds and smells which he had known intimately as a boy: the pungent scent of smoke rising through a tipi's smokehole, the sight of an Indian boy of no more than nine or ten years old tending the camp's horses some distance from the nearest tipi, the sound of someone calling out that a stranger had come into the camp with Hears Thunder—a white stranger.

But something was bothering Gabe as he rode on and people began to emerge from tipis to welcome Hears Thunder and to see the stranger aboard the horse whose hide the bright sun was turning to the color of blood. Something, yes—but what?

And then he knew. As familiar as it all was, this Lakota camp with its tipis and voices speaking the Lakota language, was also different, different in significant ways, he saw, from the camps of his boyhood among the People.

There were, for example, no women scraping the hides of buffalo free of fur. Neither were there any cooking fires visible anywhere. The children—they were not the full-bodied children he had played with years ago in just such a camp. Many of them instead, he saw with a sharp pang of sorrow, were the children of deprivation if not outright starvation. Bigbellied and yet gaunt, they stared listlessly up at him as he passed by.

In this camp, the children, as far as he could see, played no games. They did not play the Sticking-together Game as he had, whipping his top on the ice of a pond or river along with the other boys and girls of his age to see which of their tops—often it was his— could outbump and outspin all the others. Here no children sledded on bowed buffalo ribs or, in very cold weather such as January often brought, on sheets of rawhide.

But he noted that many of the children's ears were pierced and some of them wore earrings. He remembered the time of his own ear-piercing, done, as Lakota custom dictated, by a warrior who had struck coup, a brave man, he recalled, named Seven Stars who had caused him almost no pain during the ear-piercing process.

Automatically, his left hand rose and pulled on his ear. The hole in its lobe had long since closed up as had the one in his right ear. He dropped his hand.

"Hiieeee!"

The shrill cry had come from the throat of a young woman whom Gabe judged to be in her early twenties as she raced with arms outstretched in welcome toward Hears Thunder, a broad smile on her darkly beautiful face, the fringe on her beaded buckskin dress flying out behind her as she ran.

He drew rein as Hears Thunder halted just ahead of him and watched the woman throw her arms around Hears Thunder and bury her face against his chest.

As the pair embraced, Hears Thunder whispered words Gabe could not hear in the woman's ear. Then she drew back and called out a name—Warm Blanket. She beckoned. Then she walked back to where a group of children stood clustered close together. She took the arm of a young girl about thirteen years old and led her over to where Hears Thunder stood with his arms folded and a smile on his face.

The woman told Warm Blanket to properly greet her uncle which the girl did, her eyes shifting afterward to Gabe and then quickly away, the eyes of a shy animal in the face of what might be or become danger. But in those bright eyes Gabe had seen the emerging woman's boldness that lurked behind the mask of the shy child.

"My sister," Hears Thunder said to Gabe, indicating the woman. "Sky Walking Woman."

Gabe dismounted and greeted Sky Walking Woman who looked down at the ground instead of at him in the polite way such a meeting demanded. She in turn said,

"My daughter, Warm Blanket. Child, say hello to the white man."

Warm Blanket murmured a greeting.

"My name is Gabe Conrad," Gabe told her and her mother.

"His name is also Long Rider," Hears Thunder said loud enough for the gathered crowd to hear.

Murmurs rose as people turned to one another and repeated the name, Long Rider, which rippled through the crowd and brought with it looks of awe from eyes full of wonder that stared at Gabe boldly, Lakota manners forgotten in the surprise of the moment and the meeting that had just brought a legend to life on an otherwise ordinary day in an otherwise ordinary Lakota camp.

"Come, Long Rider," Hears Thunder said. "We go to my tipi. Warm Blanket, take Long Rider's horse and put it with the others."

As Warm Blanket, without looking at Gabe, took the reins of his sorrel and began to lead the horse away to the spot outside the camp where the other horses were being grazed, Gabe followed Hears Thunder and Sky Walking Woman to a tipi on the far side of the camp.

Hears Thunder did not bother to shake the bear-claw rattle that hung at the tipi's entrance before entering which told Gabe that no one was inside the shelter. He followed Hears Thunder and his sister into the tipi, walking to the left as was the custom for an invited guest and then sitting crosslegged on the bed Hears Thunder gestured toward.

"Are you hungry, my brother?" Sky Walking Woman asked. "May I get you something to eat, Long Rider?" she asked Gabe.

When both men nodded, she left the tipi. When she

returned a few minutes later, she was carrying a small buckskin bag which she placed in the center of the dirt floor. Then, kneeling, she proceeded to build a fire. Over it, she placed an iron tripod from which she hung a blackened kettle. Once again she left the tipi, returning minutes later with water which she poured into the kettle.

"I bring you no money this time," Hears Thunder told her as he rummaged among the blankets and buffalo robes piled high behind the bed on which he had seated himself crosslegged.

Sky Walking Woman said nothing.

Hears Thunder found what he had been searching for—his pipe, which was decorated near its stone bowl with a miniature effigy of a buffalo calf, and a buckskin pouch.

"You say nothing," he remarked to his sister as he took *kinnikinnick*, a blend of tobacco and herbs, from his pouch and filled the stone bowl of his pipe with the aromatic mixture.

"It is not my place to speak of what you do in the white man's world," Sky Woman declared as she continued skinning the sweet potatoes and turnips she had taken from her buckskin bag and dropping them into the kettle.

Hears Thunder took a brand from the fire and lit his pipe. He inhaled and then, after blowing a cloud of smoke toward the fire, handed the pipe to Gabe who took it, inhaled, and blew smoke in the four directions of the compass.

"White men in town make sport of me," Hears Thunder told his sister. "Two men. They had guns."

Sky Walking Woman glanced at her brother, a worried look on her face.

"They did me no harm," Hears Thunder quickly assured her. "Long Rider came and stopped the sport. He knew me for one of the Lakota, he told me, because of the tattoo on my forehead."

Gabe, as he handed the pipe back to Hears Thunder, said to Sky Walking Woman, "I told your brother that I knew what the mark meant. That it would protect him from *Hihan Kara*, the Owl Maker, should the men who were bothering him kill him."

"It is a joke, sister," said Hears Thunder as he noticed the frown on Sky Walking Woman's face. "Long Rider would not let the men kill me. Even if they had, the tattoo would keep *Hihan Kara* from throwing me off the Spirit Trail as I made my way to the Land of Many Lodges."

"I hope the old woman, *Hihan Kara*, when she examines me on the day that I walk the Spirit Trail," Gabe said lightly, "finds my mark. I don't relish being pushed off the Spirit Trail in the sky by her and having to spend the rest of eternity wandering the earth as a ghost."

"You have a tattoo that will save you from her?" Hears Thunder inquired.

Gabe stretched out his arm so that his right wrist was visible beneath his coat. On the inside of his wrist was tattooed a small blue dot.

"That ought to keep me safe and let me get to the Land of Many Lodges," he said. "What really worries me though isn't *Hihan Kara* but *Tate*, the Wind. *Tate's* liable to blow me off the Spirit Trail before I ever get a chance to be judged by *Skan*, the Sky."

The names of the Lakota's supernatural beings came easily to Gabe's lips, surprising him since he had thought little and talked less of them to anyone for many long years. Now he knew the Spirit Trail as the Milky Way. Now the sky was not *Skan* but merely the sky and he knew the wind by no other name than that—the wind. A sense of melancholy, a sense of something precious lost, swept over him momentarily but was driven away by Sky Walking Woman's next words.

"Thank you, Long Rider, for saving the life of my beloved brother."

"I'm not sure that's what I did. It was more like stopping a pair of bees from stinging your brother though I suppose it could have gotten worse than that if I hadn't stepped in. Anyway, you're welcome, Sky Walking Woman."

"Go outside," she said to her brother, "and bring Warm Blanket back here. The food is almost ready."

When Hears Thunder had put out his pipe and left the tipi, Gabe studied Sky Walking Woman as she stirred the contents of the kettle with a long spoon made from a buffalo bone. An attractive woman, he thought. Maybe not a beauty but nowhere near ugly. A solid body. Full breasts. Long slender legs.

"Where is your husband?" he asked.

"In the Land of Many Lodges," Sky Walking Woman replied. "His horse fell on him and killed him in the Moon of Ripe Plums."

"I'm sorry to hear that. You must miss him."

Sky Walking Woman glanced at Gabe and then back at the food she was stirring in the kettle. "I miss him very much. They tell me in time the pain I feel will go away. Maybe that is so. I hope it is so. I feel an emptiness inside me. A hole in my heart. My husband, White Eagle, was a good man. I loved him even when he stayed away from me to gamble. He loved to play Moccasins."

Sky Walking Woman stopped stirring, and looked away from the fire. "White Eagle would gamble for hours—even days—at a time. I would go and say to him, 'Come home.' He would say to me, 'Go home.' *Yumni* loved my husband as much as I did." Gabe smiled at Sky Walking Woman's reference to *Yumni*, the god of games who, the People said, was pleased when they wagered on games of chance like Moccasins.

"Here we are," declared Hears Thunder as he entered the tipi with Warm Blanket.

Sky Walking Woman, her reverie broken into by their arrival, began to spoon the contents of the kettle into bowls, which she passed out to the others.

Gabe ate his boiled sweet potatoes and turnips with relish to satisfy the hunger he had not been conscious of until he had the bowl of food in his hand.

"Where did you get these vegetables?" Hears Thunder asked his sister.

"I borrowed them from Deer Alone. She said she had more than enough to feed her own family and I was welcome to them."

Hears Thunder snorted derisively. "You know she lied to you. Deer Alone is a generous woman but as poor as we are." To Gabe, he said, "See what my sister and I have come to. We are beggars now. We beg food of the white man and, when he fails to provide for us, we must go to friends and beg food from them. I, who as a boy was trained to be a hunter and a warrior, am now but a beggar."

For a time no one spoke.

Finally, Gabe said, "These are hard times for the People. When I dreamed of buffalo, I dreamed that *Tatanka* would always provide for us. It was not to be. The white hunters have seen to that."

Sky Walking Woman, sitting on one of the tipi's beds with her legs to one side as was the custom for women, studied Gabe for a moment. "You are a Buffalo Dreamer?"

"Yes, I am."

Sky Walking Woman's gaze shifted from Gabe to Warm Blanket who was making slurping noises as she spooned the vegetable stew into her mouth. She looked up and met her mother's thoughtful gaze.

Warm Blanket said, "Painted Pony told me he dreamed of Elk not long ago."

"My daughter," said Sky Walking Woman, "links everything that is said or done to boys."

"Mother, I do not!" Warm Blanket protested.

"She is of that age," Sky Walking Woman added with another glance at Gabe.

They talked then of many things. Of what had been happening on the reservation, about the soldiers that Hears Thunder stated were "like the locusts that come in swarms," of the Ghost Dance, and of what, if anything, would stop the white tide that was flowing steadily and inexorably westward from drowning the red people in its dangerous path.

It was late when Hears Thunder announced that he would take Gabe to meet with Sitting Bull the next morning and that he was now going to bed as Warm Blanket had done hours earlier.

Gabe glanced up at the open smokehole at the top of the tipi and saw a single star shining through the aperture. "I think I'll take a walk around outside before I turn in," he said. "It's been a long time since I spent a night in a Lakota camp. I want to get the feeling of it here—" he touched his chest, "and here—" he tapped his forehead, "—so I won't soon forget it." He rose and circled to the right in the proper way for leaving a tipi.

Once outside, he stretched and drew in deep breaths of cold air that refreshed him after the somewhat close atmosphere of the tipi. He walked through the camp, nodding to the occasional person he met in the starlit night, silently reveling in the feeling of being where he belonged, if only for a while. He completed his circuit of the camp and began to double back, passing a prowling dog on his way, the faint orange light filtering through the tipis' hide coverings making them glow like beacons in the darkness. He heard the sound of voices coming from inside some of the shelters. Laughter. A baby crying. He walked on.

And almost collided with a figure moving silently among the tipis, a figure wrapped in a blanket that covered both head and body.

He stepped backward, begging the person's pardon for having been so clumsy, when the blanket was drawn away from the person's head he found himself staring into the starlit face of Sky Walking Woman.

"This is a surprise," he said, smiling. "I didn't expect to see you out here. I thought you'd have long since bedded down for the night."

"I tried to sleep but I couldn't."

"So you came out here to get some fresh air before trying again to get some sleep."

"Yes." Sky Walking Woman looked down at the ground. She wrapped the blanket tighter around her. "No."

"Yes? No?" Gabe frowned. "I don't follow you."

"I didn't come out here for fresh air," Sky Walking Woman told him in a small voice, one that was almost inaudible.

Gabe, puzzled, said, "Come on. I'll walk back with you."

She shook her head.

"It's cold and going to be colder before this night's done."

"I came out here to find you."

Sky Walking Woman's words suddenly assumed a provocative meaning in Gabe's mind. But no, he told himself. You're imagining things. Making things fit the way you'd like them to be. The lady just wants to be friendly. To have a talk. She's got something on her mind . . .

"White Eagle—my husband has been dead for four moons, as I told you," Sky Walking Woman murmured, her eyes still on the ground. "I have missed him." She looked up into Gabe's eyes. "I have missed him in many ways. A woman—it is not good for a woman to be without a man. Did you know that?"

"I—well, I suppose—"

"Neither is it good for a man—a man like you—to be without a woman. Did you know that?"

Gabe knew it. But he didn't know how to answer the question Sky Walking Woman had posed for him. If he admitted to the need for a woman that he had felt for a long time and was feeling now at this very moment, it might sound, he thought, crude or rude or . . .

"I should not talk like this to you. It is not good. It shames the memory of my husband."

"Hey, now, that's not true. What it is is it's just the natural way of things. My guess is that if White Eagle's looking down on us tonight from the Land of Many Lodges, he understands full well what you're feeling and why you came out here tonight."

Sky Walking Woman looked up at the sky that was

thick with stars. "See there," she said softly and pointed.

Gabe looked up at the Milky Way she had pointed to. "The Spirit Trail."

"I do not want to walk it without ever again having known love or the touch of a man's hands, the fire of his body against mine. Until tonight, I saw no man that would make me feel as I do now or say the things I have just said to you. I have been with no man. But then you came, Long Rider, and I saw—" Leaving her sentence unfinished, Sky Walking Woman reached out from beneath the blanket that covered her and gently touched Gabe's face with the tips of her fingers.

He reached out and drew her to him, held her there against him, feeling desire growing within him, feeling passion stir in his groin to harden his shaft.

"Is Hears Thunder still asleep?" he whispered hoarsely. "Warm Blanket, does she sleep too?"

"They were asleep when I left the tipi. But they might wake up and hear us if we were to go there."

"When I lived with the Lakota, I more than once lifted the side of a tipi during the night to steal inside to take a girl who had encouraged me by making calf eyes at me at a Night Dance. We could be quiet and not wake them."

Sky Walking Woman shook her head. "There is a tipi—that one over there. It is empty. It belongs—it belonged to an old man who lived there alone, Strong Heart. He died. We could go there."

"And ask the old man's blessing for the fire that burns within both of us tonight."

"Yes. Ask Strong Heart's blessing and—White Eagle's."

Gabe took Sky Walking Woman by the hand and led

her to the empty tipi she had pointed out. They entered
it and in the utter darkness inside embraced once again.

"I'll build a fire," Gabe said and bent down, feeling
about until he found the fire pit that had been dug in
the ground. He found some kindling and lit a match.
Soon he had a low fire burning. He stood up and looked
around. No bed. No blankets. The tipi was empty.

Sky Walking Woman, as if sensing what he was
thinking, said, "All Strong Heart owned was placed
with him on his burial scaffold in a tree not far from
camp."

"We've got this," Gabe said, touching the blanket
Sky Walking Woman wore. "And this," he added,
touching his buffalo coat.

They used his coat to cover themselves as they lay
on Sky Walking Woman's blanket. They shuffled about
beneath Gabe's coat until they had most of their clothes
off, then they came together, driven by desire that soon
became a wild delight.

Their coupling was complete almost at once. Sky
Walking Woman was wet and Gabe, fully aroused,
eased into her easily and began to thrust, his pelvis
plunging, rising and falling, and she, her arms wrapped
around him and her legs encircling his thighs, rose up
to meet him, withdrew, and rose again in a frenzied
rhythm that spoke silently but eloquently of her previ-
ous abstinence and the power of her desire.

It went on for some time, Gabe holding back, wanting to be sure to give pleasure as well as to take it. He
felt the blood begin to pound in his temples. He felt
the world shrink and become centered in his genitals,
all thought and feeling focused there.

Sky Walking Woman let out a little cry. Her finger-
nails raked Gabe's naked back, nearly drawing blood.

Her legs tightened around his, holding him a willing prisoner against her hot body that banished the chill of the air in the tipi.

As she climaxed beneath him, Gabe let fall the barrier to his own pleasure he had erected and, his body spasming, he flooded her with his seed.

She moaned and continued to hold him tightly, her neck arched and her head thrown backward.

Moments later, he lay there, panting and feeling more relaxed than he had in a very long time. Her fingers played across his back, a silent symphony that caused him to shiver with pleasure.

"Sky Walking Woman," he murmured, her name an erotic incantation on his lips.

"Long Rider," she whispered and sighed. "Buffalo Dreamer."

He withdrew from her and lay by her side, one arm wrapped around her to hold her close to him. "If you had not come to me tonight I would have made medicine to give me power over you as Buffalo Dreamers can do."

"I know you can make strong medicine. I have seen Buffalo Dreamers make medicine for young men so that they will have much power over young girls."

"Did it work?"

"In one case I know about from my own experience, yes, it did work. I was the girl and the young man was White Eagle."

"What medicine did the Buffalo Dreamer make so that White Eagle might win you?"

"He made for White Eagle a Big Twisted Flute."

Gabe smiled and kissed Sky Walking Woman on the neck. An image of the Big Twisted Flute floated through his mind, the wind instrument that was traditionally made of cedar and decorated with the effigy of a horse, the animal that was the most ardent of lovers.

"Did the shaman also make the music that White Eagle must play on the flute to win women?" Gabe asked, thinking of the times he had made Big Twisted Flutes for friends, and also given them the music he had heard in a dream so that they might be successful in love.

"He did and it was irresistible."

"It nearly always is."

"When White Eagle would play the flute near my parents' tipi, I would become very nervous. Like a mare when a rogue stallion is nearby. One night I could resist its call no longer. I waited until my parents were asleep and then crept outside and went to White Eagle, who was waiting for me in a grove of quaking aspens. I remember it all so well. It was a night during the Moon of Strawberries and the scent of flowers was in the air. So was the scent of love.

"White Eagle stopped playing and took me by the hand. He led me to the lodge of the shaman, a Buffalo Dreamer like you, who had made the Big Twisted Flute for him. Once there, the shaman blew the smoke of some herbs he had burned into my face and I went away from myself."

Gabe stroked Sky Walking Woman's chin, her neck, then her breasts, recalling the trances into which women had fallen as a result of the medicine made by the shaman who had carved the Big Twisted Flute which resembled nothing so much in its construction as an erect male member.

"When I awoke," Sky Walking Woman continued, in a dreamy voice, "and saw where I was and realized what had happened, I knew I was now married to White

Eagle. My parents considered what had happened an elopement which, in a way, it was. I eloped that magical night into another world and when I returned to this one I belonged to White Eagle as a result of the shaman's magic. Next day, White Eagle paid a bride's price—five ponies—to my parents.''

"A generous man, your husband."

"He said I was worth even more than what he had paid,'' Sky Walking Woman said softly, shyly.

They lay together then, their hot bodies gradually cooling, gently touching one another to say tender things without using any words at all.

Some time later, Sky Walking Woman said, "I would have you do something for me for which I am willing to pay any price you see fit to charge.''

"What do you have in mind?"

"Warm Blanket bled for the first time only two days ago. It is the time of her first menses.''

"I see," Gabe said, sure he knew now what Sky Walking Woman wanted him to do. "You want me to do a Buffalo Sing for her.''

"I will pay."

"You will not. I will do it because you asked me to do it. I need no payment.''

"You are generous."

"I am your friend."

"And you are a Buffalo Dreamer."

"Buffalo, protector of young girls and the patron of female virtues, will bring good fortune to Warm Blanket. I am sure of it.''

"When will you do it?"

"I cannot tell you that for sure. I go in the morning to meet with Sitting Bull. We will talk. Then I plan to go to the agency to speak to Agent McLaughlin. I have things to say to that man and I want to hear him say things to me—things that will explain, if such things can be explained, why it is the People go hungry under his care. Maybe tomorrow night we can do it if I return from the agency in time. Or the night after tomorrow night if I do not return in time.''

''I will make ready for the ceremony,'' Sky Walking Woman declared, a lilt in her voice now, an eagerness that had not been there before. ''Soon my daughter will be a Buffalo Woman,'' she added. ''I must gather gifts to give to the guests who will come to the Sing in honour of Warm Blanket's passage into womanhood. I must cook for those who come to visit. There is so much I must do. I feel as if I want to jump up right now and begin.''

''Don't,'' Gabe whispered into her ear. ''Don't go. Not yet. I know you have many things to do before the Sing. But so do we have many things to do together here and now before *Wi*, the Sun, returns and routs us from our pleasures.''

Together, they did the many things Gabe had spoken of as the hours passed and the night grew old and died.

CHAPTER FOUR

In the morning, after only an hour's sleep, Gabe rose to find a fire already burning in Hears Thunder's tipi. He nodded a greeting to Sky Walking Woman who was tending the fire and to Hears Thunder and Warm Blanket who were both seated beside it.

"I'll go get some food I brought," he told them and left the tipi.

Once outside, he found the herd boy tending the horses and asked him where his gear was. The boy pointed and Gabe went over to where his saddle was piled beside his other gear. He rummaged about among his belongings and came up with the food he had bought in the town across the Missouri River.

When he returned with it, he gave it all to Sky Walking Woman who thanked him profusely and proceeded to open the cans of tomatoes, pouring their contents into the kettle hanging above the fire. Into the kettle also went some of Gabe's dried apples. The salt pork he had brought she speared with an iron prong and held over the flames to cook it.

"We eat," Hears Thunder said, "then we go to Sitting Bull."

When the morning meal had been consumed, Gabe bade goodbye to Sky Walking Woman and Warm Blanket and followed Hears Thunder from the tipi to the lodge of Sitting Bull.

There Hears Thunder thumped a hand on the tipi and in response a male voice called out to invite them to come in.

Gabe followed Hears Thunder into the tipi. He moved to the right behind Hears Thunder and then halted to stand facing the aging Sitting Bull who sat on the far side of a low fire.

The chief was seated crosslegged on a buffalo robe spread on the ground, his arms folded across his chest. His slouch hat sat on the robe next to his right foot. He wore a buffalo fur vest over a flannel shirt. His buckskin trousers were grease-stained and his moccasins showed signs of wear.

His black hair was bound by rawhide thongs and hung in two clusters across his massive chest. His face was dominated by the sharp cheekbones on his round face. His black eyes were clear and they studied Gabe with undisguised interest. Lines were deeply etched in his face just above the bridge of his large nose and running also from his nostrils to the outer edges of his thin lips.

He directed the two men to seats—Gabe to the place of honor in the tipi, the *catku*, which was located directly across from the entrance.

When he and Hears Thunder had seated themselves crosslegged in their appointed places, Sitting Bull said, "We will smoke."

He proceeded to fill the bowl of a pipe, which had been made from a hollowed-out red stone, with *chan-shasha*, willow bark, and light it.

Silence dominated the tipi as the pipe was passed back and forth among the three men and the smoke drifted up and out of the smokehole. Nearly ten minutes passed before the tobacco in the pipe had been consumed and Sitting Bull had set it aside. Then, he said, "I was told last night that the Oglala, Long Rider, he who is spoken of around many Lakota campfires, had come to this camp. Sitting Bull welcomes him."

"I am glad to be here," Gabe said.

"Why have you come among the Hunkpapa, Long Rider?" Sitting Bull inquired.

"I have heard white men speak of the Ghost Dance religion. I came to learn about it."

"There is little to learn. Ghost Dancers try to visit the Land of Many Lodges without dying in order to do so. They dance to bring a new day to the People's many council fires. They say they will bring back the buffalo. They believe the white men will be banished from our land by their dances and their songs. They long for the coming of the promised messiah. That is all. I have said it."

Hears Thunder said, "Long Rider and I met in the town where I had gone to work to earn the white man's money." He proceeded to tell Sitting Bull about his encounter with Gabe.

When he had finished, Sitting Bull said, "You were always a friend to the People, Long Rider. I have heard your uncle, Red Cloud, tell of your long ride that bitter winter to save some of the People from the pony soldiers. I have heard him tell of how you lived among us until your mother sent you away when you had fourteen years. Were you glad to go?''

"No," Gabe answered, thinking how Sitting Bull was not only incisive in his thinking but quick to unsettle a man with his probing questions.

"Explain."

"I wanted to remain where I believed I belonged. Where I had family and friends. But my mother—even the brave who took her to wife after the death of my father—"

"Little Wound," Sitting Bull interjected.

Gabe nodded. "Even he thought I should go out into the white man's world and learn how to live there. I hated going and I hated my mother for making me go. But as the years went by I learned that she was right to have done so. I had to learn to live in the world in which I did not grow up."

"Uh," Sitting Bull grunted. "It would be well if we were all to do what you have done. Maybe then, when we have learned how to live in a world that is not ours, we will be allowed to survive. But I think that is not to be. The white man does not want us in his world; he wants us shut up on his reservations while he goes about making *Maka*, the Earth, sad as he plunders what the god has given us. *Wi*, the Sun, looks down, with sorrow on the white hunters who have left the buffalo's bones to rot beneath *Wi's* hot eye, wanting, as they do, only the robes, not the flesh, not the sinew, not the hooves that can be boiled into glue, not the horns that can become powder flasks, not the berry bags that can be made from the hide of an unborn calf—it is enough. I talk too much."

"You speak the truth," Hears Thunder said dolefully.

"A worrisome truth," Gabe said, causing Sitting Bull to nod.

"Do you see your uncle often?" the chief then asked him.

"I have not seen Red Cloud since we fought together on the Bozeman Trail against the pony soldiers."

"I have heard of you and how you fought in that time. It was you who spoke out so strongly in favor of Red Cloud's strategy, which was supported as strongly by Crazy Horse."

"That is so. I had the honor in those years of becoming a friend to Crazy Horse and an advisor to Red Cloud."

"I have also heard how your mother, Amelia, and your young wife, Yellow Buckskin Girl, were killed by the white soldier."

Captain Stanley Price.

The man's face burns now in Gabe's tormented memory. The hatred he still has for the man silently savages him. He remembers the time he went in search of his mother, Amelia Conrad, and her Oglala husband, Little Wound, who, he had learned had gone to visit some of Little Wound's relatives living then among the Northern Arapaho on the Tongue River. When he arrived at the camp, the Cheyenne warrior, Little Horse, warned the residents of the camp that he has seen soldiers approaching from the south.

But, Gabe recalls with sorrow, few then believed that the soldiers would dare to invade the Sioux stronghold on the river. He recalls the joyful reunion with his mother that took place only hours before the white pony soldiers attacked the Arapaho camp.

Images, all of them ugly, roil in his mind now as he relives the terrible scenes that took place during that attack. The men fighting off the pony soldiers—trying to. The women fighting just as hard and as well, his mother foremost among them. Captain Price bearing down on Amelia Conrad. Her firing at him—and missing. Price plunging his saber into Amelia's body, killing her. Gabe's pain intensifies as he recalls the killing, also by Price, of Yellow Buckskin Girl the wife he had loved with all his heart, the wife now lost to him forever.

Afterward, when the attack is over . . .

A truly terrible scene.

Smoke filled the air around him from burning tipis. Smoke that choked him, mixed with his tears to stain his face. The stench of burned hides that were once lodges and of burned bodies that were once human beings. He hears again the screams of the wounded, trapped in their agony. The sound of others singing their death songs. He sees again the survivors wandering forlornly among the dead, crying out in anguish when they find a slaughtered loved one.

"—the Land of Many Lodges."

Gabe hears Sitting Bull's words but they register only vaguely in his consciousness. He opens his eyes, which he had not realized he had closed as memory swept down upon him, and once again sees Sitting Bull. "I am sorry," he murmurs. "I was remembering—I did not hear what you were saying."

"I spoke of your mother and your wife. I said you must not mourn them any longer. They are at peace in the Land of Many Lodges. There they await you. While they wait, they do not hunger or thirst but are content."

Gabe nodded, not trusting himself to speak.

Hears Thunder said, "My sister told me this morning

that Long Rider will perform the Buffalo Sing ceremony for my niece, Warm Blanket.''

Sitting Bull smiled. ''I grow old. When did Warm
Blanket become a woman? The last time I looked—was
it yesterday? The day before? The last time I looked at
your niece, she was a child chasing butterflies through
the long grass.''

It was Hears Thunder's turn to smile. ''We all grow
old, Sitting Bull. My niece is a woman now. My sister
told me to be sure to invite you to the ceremony.''

''I consider it an honor to be invited. Thank Sky
Walking Woman for me and tell Warm Blanket that I
said I am sure she will be as beautiful as the brightest
star in *Skan*, the Sky, when the Buffalo Sing is over and
she begins to wear her hair in the way of a woman.
When is the Buffalo Sing to take place?''

With a glance, Hears Thunder turned the question in
Gabe's direction.

''When I return from the agency,'' he answered.

Sitting Bull snorted. ''The agency. Why do you go
there? There is nothing there but talk and more talk.
No beef. No flour or salt. You waste your time going
there, Long Rider.''

''That may be so. But I decided to have myself a talk
with Agent McLaughlin. From everything I've heard
he's a good man who tries his best to do his job well.''

''He believes me to be his enemy,'' Sitting Bull stated
solemnly.

Gabe was about to ask why when Sitting Bull answered his unspoken question.

''He thinks I am a leader of the Ghost Dance religion
which he fears, as do all whites who, like him, do not
understand it. That is because there have been Ghost
Dances held here by my people, the Hunkpapa. But I

am not a leader of the dance. To speak the truth to you, I do not believe in it—not with my whole heart. Still, I have sent word to McLaughlin that I wish to attend, as do many others here in camp, a Ghost Dance that is to be held by Chief Big Foot at his camp on the Cheyenne River Reservation. Since McLaughlin has forbidden me to hold Ghost Dances here, I will go where they are held.''

"Has McLaughlin given you permission to go?" Gabe asked.

Sitting Bull shook his head. "It is likely he will refuse me permission to leave the reservation." A smile. "But I will go anyway." The smile was replaced by a stern expression and a pair of eyes in which a bright fire smoldered. "Long Rider, did you ever think the Lakota would come to such a pass? That we would ever have to petition an invader for permission to roam at will on our own lands in our own country?"

"I did not."

When Sitting Bull said nothing, Gabe said, "I did not know the Ghost Dance had reached the Miniconjou."

"It is everywhere today," Hears Thunder declared. "That may be good; that may be bad."

Gabe rose. "I thank you, Sitting Bull, for talking to me. I will see you at the Buffalo Sing."

Sitting Bull also rose. "When you see McLaughlin, tell him that Sitting Bull waits for word from him concerning my planned journey south."

"I will tell him."

It was late in the afternoon when Gabe came within sight of the Standing Rock agency. He rode across a stretch of flatland that was matted with withered grama grass and then past a grove of white pines and finally in among the agency's wooden buildings.

White men moved into and out of the buildings. There were no women in sight. Specifically, no Lorelei Adams was in sight, though Gabe looked for her. A few Indians sat stoically silent on the verandas of some of the buildings or on the ground in front of shabby tipis sprouting near them.

Gabe asked a passing man where the agency headquarters was and was directed to a building in the center of the settlement. He walked his horse there, dismounted, and wrapped his reins around a hitchrail.

He went inside and up to the nattily-uniformed Indian policeman who was seated behind a desk gathering official-looking papers into a neat pile.

When the man neither looked up nor spoke to him, Gabe said, "I'm here to see McLaughlin. He in there?" He pointed to a door behind the policeman.

When he still received no answer, he reached out and seized the policeman by the lapels of his uniform coat and hauled the startled man to his feet.

"I asked you a question. I want an answer."

"Let me go!"

Gabe didn't. Instead, he leaped up on the desk and then down on the other side of it. He held the man inches away from his own body and shook him violently. "Now you contemptuous sonofabitch, are you going to answer me?"

"He's in there. But he's busy. You can't see Agent McLaughlin without an appointment."

"Your skin is red but your mind and your heart are as white as any snow I've ever seen. You push papers around and spout babble about appointments and such as good as—maybe better than—any white man I've ever met. McLaughlin's trained his Lakota dogs well, it looks like to me. They bark just like they've been taught to. Now, what I'm wondering is do they know how to bite.''

The policeman slammed a stony fist into Gabe's groin, causing Gabe to cry out in pain and reflexively loosen his hold on his prisoner.

The policeman tore himself free of Gabe's grip and swung his left fist which landed with a bone-jarring crack on Gabe's right cheekbone.

Gabe danced backward out of the policeman's reach as he clutched his genitals with both hands and gasped for breath. He ducked as the policeman lunged for him and then went in under the man's outstretched arms, butting his head up against his attacker's gut and knocking the wind out of the man.

The policeman staggered backward and collided with the desk. Gabe, recovering his balance and trying hard to ignore the pain in his groin, sprang forward and threw a powerful roundhouse right which slammed into the policeman's solar plexus just beneath the juncture of the man's ribs.

He let out a loud grunt and doubled over. Gabe brought his knee up. It cracked against the man's lower jaw. The policeman's head was thrown up from the force of the blow and then it swung down again as he lost consciousness and fell to the floor by Gabe's boots.

At the same instant the door behind the desk burst open and two men, one white, the other another Indian policeman, rushed into the room.

''What's the meaning of this ruckus?'' cried the white man, who was heavyset and walrus-mustached. His florid face grew even redder as he stared at the downed policeman and then at Gabe, anger in his eyes.

"This man—" Gabe pointed to the fallen policeman, "—treated me like I was beneath his notice when I came in here and asked him just as polite as you please if I could see the Indian Agent."

"I am the Indian Agent," the white man declared hotly. "Do you always react so violently if you feel you have been mistreated by someone?"

"Usually, yes. It's one of my many faults. So you're McLaughlin."

"I am. Who, may I ask, are you?"

"Name's Gabe Conrad."

"Well, Mr. Conrad I don't know you but I do know this about you. You are most obviously a very hot-headed man."

"That's because I've seen things in the last day or so that are enough to make any man hotheaded. I've seen hungry—damn near starving—Lakota children at Sitting Bull's camp with bellies bulging like big balloons underneath their clothes and I've seen people there who, for want of food, would make a skeleton fresh-dug out of a grave look like the picture of health. When I was leaving the camp this morning to come here, I saw women gathering grass. When I questioned them about what they were doing and why, they told me they intended to boil the grass they'd cleaned and eat it. *Grass*, McLaughlin! You want me to go on and tell you some more reasons why I'm so goddamed hotheaded as you just pointed out?"

McLaughlin, the fire going out of his eyes, sighed. "I know," he said, shaking his head sorrowfully. "The beef ration, at the present time, is far from sufficient to meet the needs of the Indians. Congress, in its infinite wisdom, has seen fit to reduce the allocation of beef by over one-half. From 580,600 pounds last year to only

209,000 pounds this year. That has led to many of our former beef contractors being unwilling to sell beef to us any longer. Why should they when they can sell steadily and in greater quantities to the more dependable Eastern markets? And, I must add, at a far better per-head price than the government is willing to pay them. That, in turn, results in this agency being able to obtain even *less* than the authorized monthly quota authorized by Congress." McLaughlin paused, eyeing Gabe speculatively. "What is your interest in this matter, Mr. Conrad?"

Before Gabe could reply, the policeman on the floor by his feet groaned and sat up. Gabe bent down and helped the man to his feet. Once erect, he dusted himself off and glared at Gabe.

"This man," said McLaughlin, "is Sergeant Red Tomahawk. This other officer—" he indicated the stolid, well-built man standing at his side, "—is Lieutenant Henry Bull Head. Both are part of the agency's police force, as I'm sure you can tell from their uniforms."

Ignoring both men, Gabe said, "To answer your question, McLaughlin, my interest in the food supply problems the Hunkpapa are having stems from the fact that those people are my friends and I'm a man who does what he can to help his friends when he sees that they're in trouble."

"I understand."

"What can you do about getting more food to them?"

"I'm afraid there is very little I can do that I have not already done. I have written letters to congressmen and to senators explaining the plight of the Indians. I have received only polite replies and vague promises."

"But no increased allotments?"

"No increased allotments."

"You've heard it said that some folk think the only good Indian is a dead Indian," Gabe said, bitterness sharpening his tone. "Well, in my opinion, the only good politician is a dead politician."

To Gabe's surprise, McLaughlin smiled faintly. "Come into my office, Mr. Conrad. We can continue our talk there. Henry, I won't be needing you and Red Tomahawk anymore."

As Gabe followed McLaughlin into his office, the two policemen left the building.

"Sit down, Mr. Conrad."

When both men were seated, McLaughlin said, "I know you are unhappy at what you have seen at Sitting Bull's camp and you have every right to be. But I hasten to assure you not all Indian agents are knaves and villains, Mr. Conrad. I, for one, am not. Will you believe me when I tell you I have done my level best—much more than that at times—to see to it that treaties are honored by our people—I mean white people—and that the beef ration is increased, rather than decreased?"

Gabe, the rage that had fueled his encounter with Sergeant Red Tomahawk cooling somewhat, nodded. "I've heard people say good things about you, McLaughlin. But there's another thing I wanted to talk to you about. Take it from me, you're doing yourself more harm than good by meddling in the new religion the Indians have come up with."

"The Ghost Dance, you mean."

"Yes. McLaughlin, if you and a few other well-intentioned white men would just take the time and the trouble to find out exactly what that religion's all about

there wouldn't be any need for all this fuming and fuss-
ing over it.''

"I know what it is because I have investigated and
studied it. I know the Indians do not dance as a prelude
to a violent outbreak of hostilities. But I am unable to
convince others of that fact. Fear, Mr. Conrad. Fear
stalks the land. The settlers across the river in Missouri
believe, almost to a man, that Indians will come howl-
ing into their homes any day now if the Ghost Dance
is allowed to continue. Many of them have contacted
their government representatives for help. Those men,
in turn, have seen to it that many more troops have been
sent out here to Sioux country. Why, the garrison at
Fort Yates, under the command of Colonel Drum, has
nearly doubled in size in the past two months alone—
as a direct result of the Indians' ghost dancing. The
same, I'm told, is true of Fort Bennett down on the
Cheyenne River reservation.''

"So you're fixing to use force to stop the Indians
from ghost dancing, is that it?''

"*I* am not going to use force. Not, that is, unless I
am forced to do so due to a lack of cooperation on the
part of men like Sitting Bull. It is the army that will
use force if such a tactic becomes necessary.''

"You're in favor of that, are you?''

"No, I decidedly am not, sir!'' McLaughlin answered heatedly, his face flushing. "But I must point
out to you that I serve here at the pleasure of the Indian
Commissioner in Washington. I must follow his orders,
obey his edicts. That means, at this present time, that
I have been instructed to cooperate fully with the army
in any action they see fit to take here at Standing Rock.
All Indian agents have been so directed.''

"Can't you see what's coming, McLaughlin? I can.

I can see it as clear as spring water. A clash is coming for sure, between the army and the Indians, a head-on clash. It might not happen here. It might happen down at Pine Ridge. Or on the Rosebud reservation. But it's coming sure as the sun will rise tomorrow, it is. Doesn't that make you fearful? It does me.''

"Of course I find it disturbing.''

"You spoke to me before about fear. You said the settlers across the river in Missouri were scared out of their wits by what all the ghost dancing might mean to them and their families. Well, I'm wondering has it ever occurred to you that the Indians too might be afraid of what's ahead for them. They haven't got guns—''

"Not true, Mr. Conrad,'' McLaughlin interrupted. "Some of them have guns—perhaps even a majority of them do. *Hidden* guns.''

"Well, if that's true, how come, do you think, the Indians would hide any guns they might have? I'll tell you why that might be the case. On account of they're just as afraid of what's coming down the pike as any white man over in Missouri is. Why the hell else do you think some of them have jumped their reservations and gone hightailing it into hiding in the Badlands?''

"Because they do not take well to reservation life,'' McLaughlin answered. "Because they are a nomadic people and not accustomed to being confined.''

"That's part of it. But it's not the biggest part. The biggest part is they're afraid of all the soldiers they see everywhere around them. Soldiers with guns—all kinds of guns, from sidearms to artillery pieces from what I've heard. That's enough to make any man, me included, afraid and determined to do something to save his skin and the skins of his family and friends.''

"I'm certain you are correct in your evaluation of the

current situation, Mr. Conrad. But I don't see what I can do other than to try to defuse the admittedly explosive situation in any way available to me. To that end, I have been intending to travel tomorrow to Sitting Bull's camp and have a talk with him.''

''By that I take it you mean you intend to try to talk him out of any plans he might have for doing a little ghost dancing, him and his people.''

''Yes, that is so. It is a small effort, I know. Perhaps even a pitiable one. But it is one I feel a man in my position is duty- and conscience-bound to make. I want no bloodshed.''

''Neither does Sitting Bull.''

''You're sure of that?''

''No, I'm not sure of that—or sure of anything else in this sorry stew that's started boiling in this part of the country. But I've talked with Sitting Bull and he didn't talk war with the whites to me.''

''He is, after all, an Indian and you are a white man.''

''I can see what you're driving at McLaughlin. You think he might not have told me, a white man, about any plans he might be hatching. But what you ought to know is there's not such a rift between the Indians and me as you might think if you judge just by the different color of our skins. You see, I was raised as an Oglala. Sometimes I think I'm more Oglala than I am white.''

''And you believe Sitting Bull's intentions are peaceful?''

''I do.''

''I pray to God you're right, Mr. Conrad. For all our sakes.''

''To get back to this situation of your beef shortfall. What do you intend to do about that?''

"I've been doing all I can. I shall continue to press Congress for a more generous allotment. I am, after all, merely an administrator of a program that I had no hand in creating. Mine is, I submit to you in all honesty, a nearly untenable position, Mr. Conrad."

"I think you mean well, McLaughlin. I'm just sorry to hear how your hands are pretty much tied. I figure that hurts you and I can also see you know it hurts the Indians a whole helluva lot more."

McLaughlin nodded, his eyes cast down.

"I've heard good things said about you," Gabe told the agent. "I just hope you'll keep trying your damndest to get the Indians the food they need."

McLaughlin looked up. He rose from his desk and went to the door of his office. He opened it, looked out into the adjoining room and then, when he saw no one there, he closed the door and returned to his seat behind his desk.

"Mr. Conrad," he said, "I have been a follower of rules most of my life. Ever since my boyhood, in fact. I am not a trouble maker. I do what I am told to do by my superiors. But I will tell you this and I beg you not to repeat it to anyone. Heard by the wrong ears—it could mean my dismissal from my post here but, more importantly, it could make things more difficult for the Indians here at Standing Rock. I know that what I am about to tell you makes me sound immodest but—well, to get on with it—I have, of late, been paying the few beef contractors I have been able to persuade to sell beef to the agency a higher per-head price than the one authorized by the government. I have been taking the extra money from the operating budget of the agency, not from the nearly depleted fund designated for the purchase of beef and other supplies needed by the Indians. That act of mine might be seen by some in Washington as mismanagement at best and embezzlement at worst. I tell you this not to elicit praise from you but understanding. I am not an unfeeling man, Mr. Conrad. I may be a bit of a bureaucratic fool in your opinion but I am not uncaring nor am I blind to the plight of my fellow man as it exists right here in my own backyard, so to speak.''

Gabe stared at the agent in silence for a long minute. Then, ''I know what you are, McLaughlin. You're a decent man caught up in an indecent situation. I have never in my entire life heard a white man refer to the Indians as his 'fellow man' like you just did. That tells me how you look at things here. It says more about you than could be written down in a whole book. I want to thank you for feeling like you do and being the man you clearly are. Maybe one day you can make a difference in things here. I sure do hope you'll keep trying to.''

''Thank you for your kind words, Mr. Conrad. I promise you that I shall continue to try to do the best I can for the Indians under what have been and continue to be rather trying circumstances.''

Gabe got to his feet and held out his hand.

As he shook hands with McLaughlin, he asked, ''Where's your schoolhouse located?''

CHAPTER FIVE

Gabe opened the door in the building that housed both the school and the pupils' living quarters and stepped inside, expecting to find himself in the midst of a mob of children. But he saw no children, who, he guessed, were gone since it was late in the afternoon, and their studies were finished for the day. There was only Lorelei Adams who stood with her back to him as she chalked a series of sums on the blackboard.

He stood watching her, admiring the flare of her hips, her narrow waist, the delicacy of her hand that held the chalk. There was no doubt about it. Lorelei Adams was a decidedly attractive woman. He started up the aisle that separated rows of desks. The thudding of his boots on the puncheon floor caused an obviously startled Lorelei to turn quickly to face him.

"Oh," she said, flustered. "Oh, it's you Mr. Conrad."

"I'm glad you haven't forgotten my name, Miss Adams."

"No, I haven't forgotten you, Mr. Conrad," Lorelei said and Gabe did not miss the way her statement had differed in a subtle but, to him, significant way from his own. "In fact," she continued, "I was wondering what happened to you. I witnessed your encounter with those two gunmen who were harassing that Indian in town while I was waiting for the driver who would bring me here. Are you quite all right, Mr. Conrad?"

"Those two jaspers didn't bother me all that much," Gabe answered offhandedly. "Fellas like them, when a man calls their bluff, usually don't have any more guts than a snake has hips."

He matched Lorelei's sudden smile which he thought was like the sun suddenly breaking out from behind a cloud.

"What brings you here to the agency, Mr. Conrad?"

"A bit of business and pleasure both," he replied. "The business part was a talk I just had with Agent McLaughlin. The pleasure part's my visit here to see you again."

"Oh, Mr. Conrad, what a nice thing to say."

"How've you been getting on? You all settled in, are you?"

Lorelei looked around her and then back at Gabe. "Yes, I'm settled in, I suppose."

"You suppose? You mean you're not sure?"

"No, I didn't mean that. I just meant that—," Lorelei made an aimless gesture, "—there's so much to learn. About the reservation. About my pupils, the few I have. It all takes some getting used to."

"You having problems?"

Lorelei shook her head. "No, everything is fine. Fine and dandy, as they say." She turned away and began to chalk additional sums on the blackboard. She turned back again. "Forgive me, I'm being rude. Those sums can wait." She glanced at the blackboard, raised her hand that held the chalk, lowered it, looked toward the door.

"What's wrong, Miss Adams?" he asked. "Am I making you nervous? Do you want I should go?"

"No, Mr. Conrad. No, by all means stay. It's just that—it's—" Her words trailed away.

"It's that you're no liar."

Lorelei looked quizzically at Gabe who added, "This place—the Indians—none of it's what you expected, am I right? Things aren't fine and dandy as you just claimed, are they?"

Lorelei hung her head. "No, they are not. How did you know?"

"You answered my question about how things were going with a voice that was a whole lot too loud and way too quick. You seemed glad to see me at first but then you seemed to turn skittish on me all of a sudden. I figured you were lying about how things had shaped up for you here by the way you talked and I also figured you had had second thoughts about being glad to see me in case I should find out how things really were with you."

Lorelei's teeth gnawed at her lower lip. Without raising her head, she said, "You must be psychic, Mr. Conrad."

"I read you right?"

"You did. I'm sorry to say that I cannot seem to reach the children who come to the school. I am as sorry to say that there are only four of them, two boys and two girls. They won't even look at me. They don't speak English very well and I have only a rudimentary command of their language which makes things difficult. I'm afraid my days here are numbered.''

"You think the powers that be are going to fire you?''

"I think I shall have to give up this job so that they can find someone who can do it properly which I clearly cannot.''

"What you said about the kids—about how they won't look at you. That's the Indian way around strangers, Miss Adams. They don't consider it polite to look a stranger in the eye so they look away from you or down at the ground when you talk to them. As for the language problem, why don't you find somebody who can teach you some of the Lakota language? If you can arrange that, it won't be long, I'm willing to wager, before long you'll be talking Lakota like one of—''

"The *oyate ikse*. The native people.''

"Now where'd you learn that?''

"From you, Mr. Conrad. Don't you recall using that Lakota phrase when we were breakfasting in town awhile back?''

Gabe suddenly remembered. He grinned. "You just gave me an idea. I'm free this evening. Maybe I could spend a little time with you tonight to teach you some of the things you need to know about the *oyate ikse* which ought to help you understand them better. That way, maybe things would go a little bit smoother for you. I'm sure you're a good teacher. I'd hate for the Lakota to lose your services. They've lost so much else.''

"I want to remain here,'' Lorelei declared with passion in her voice. "I want to learn as much as I can about the Lakota so that I can understand them and thus be able to work well with their children. It's very important to me, Mr. Conrad. It really is.''

"Then maybe, if you're about ready to shut up shop for the day, we could go someplace—"

"There is a small house here assigned to the school-teacher. May I invite you to come there with me?"

"Sure. We'll go there and I'll teach you a few facts that might help you before I have to go back to Sitting Bull's camp. Say, that reminds me. The reason I have to go back to the camp is that I've been asked to perform a Buffalo Sing so I'll be leaving here tomorrow. Now, tomorrow's Saturday so I take it there's no school?"

"No, there isn't but what—"

"Maybe you'd like to come with me to the camp. See the Buffalo Sing. Meet some of the People. Let them get to know you. That ought to help break the ice and you're sure to learn one or two things that might help you. What do you say?"

"Well, I am free tomorrow."

"That settles it. We'll go then. First thing in the morning, if that's all right with you."

"That will be fine."

"Now let's go to your place and I'll be the teacher and you be the pupil. How's that sound to you?"

Lorelei smiled. "Wonderful, Mr. Conrad. It sounds simply wonderful."

"More coffee, Mr. Conrad?" Lorelei asked as Gabe emptied his cup.

"No, thank you, I've not got room for anything more, not even a swallow of coffee. That was one fine meal you fixed, Miss Adams, and I thank you kindly for it."

"You didn't think the biscuits were too hard?"

"They were soft as snowflakes."

Lorelei sat back in her chair and patted her lips with her napkin. She glanced at Gabe. "It's I who should be thanking you, you know."

"Why?"

"For all you've taught me during the last few hours. I just hope I can remember it all."

"Just keep the number four in mind. That's the key that ought to unlock your memory."

"I shall. Do you mind if I go over it with you one more time to be sure I've got it all?"

"Go ahead."

"The Rulers of the World game—that's what you think I should call it?"

Gabe nodded. "It'll show the four kids you're teaching that you know something about the Lakota religion. Even though you'll be turning it into a game, they'll understand that you've taken the time and trouble to learn about things that are important to them."

"You don't think it would be sacrilegious, do you? I mean making a schoolyard game out of—"

"The People live close to both their main and lesser gods. No, I don't think it would offend anybody. It's really just another way of teaching when you come right down to it. A roundabout way maybe but a workable one."

Lorelei held up the four fingers of her left hand and began to tick them off, one by one. "The Gods-Kindred number four. They are the Buffalo, the Bear, the Four Winds, and the Whirlwind."

"You can have the boys play the parts of Bear and Buffalo and the girls can be the Four Winds and Whirlwind," Gabe suggested.

"Even more amusing I think in terms of its potential

for playfulness will be a game peopled by the evil spirits. Let's see if I've got it all straight. There is *Iktomo*—''

"*Iktomi*," Gabe corrected.

"*Iktomi*," Lorelei repeated. "The first son of *Rock* and known as the Trickster. I know exactly who shall play *Iktomi* in our little playlets. His name is Cold Water. He's ten years old and a trickster if there ever was one.

"Today he tripped Small Flower. She's twelve and I think Cold Water has a crush on her."

Gabe smiled and said, "Let Small Flower play *Anog-Ite*, Two-Faced Woman, goddess of shameful things, so she can get even with Cold Water."

"And two others to play *Anog-Ite's* father, *Waziya*, the Old Man, and his wife, *Wakanaka*, the Witch."

"You've got it all straight. After a few go-rounds with these games, your scholars ought to think of you as one of their very own."

"I hope so. I truly do. I want very much to do a good job here. You've helped me immeasurably tonight, Mr. Conrad, with all the information you've given me—the Lakota phrases you've taught me and so on. Which prompts me to ask exactly what is this Buffalo Sing you are taking me to see tomorrow?"

"It's a Lakota ceremony which celebrates a young girl's entry into womanhood. It's being held for the daughter of a friend of mine. The girl's name is Warm Blanket and her mother is Sky Walking Woman."

"I'm looking forward to it."

"You've got a horse you can ride to the camp?"

"No, but Mr. McLaughlin has offered me the use of a surrey whenever I might need it."

"That'll do fine. I'll tie my horse to the back of it

and drive you to Sitting Bull's camp first thing tomorrow morning.''

''I had better get some things ready for the journey,'' Lorelei said, rising from the table.

Gabe got up and stood facing her. ''You'll want to dress warmly. Have you got a fur coat?''

''No, but I have a heavy woolen one which will do me quite well, I believe.'' Lorelei picked up the coffee pot and placed it on the stove. ''First, though, I must clean up here and then—''

Gabe rounded the table. ''I'll help you,'' he volunteered.

''Oh, that won't be necessary, Mr. Conrad. I can manage quite well on my own.''

''Can you?''

Lorelei looked into his eyes and then quickly lowered her gaze.

''There aren't many of us who can manage well on our own. Not all the time. Not for too long a time.''

''Yes, I suppose that's true.'' Lorelei gave a little laugh which betrayed her nervousness. ''You're a philosopher, Mr. Conrad.''

''No, I'm not. I'm just a man with some experience in the world is all.'' He reached for Lorelei.

He felt her flinch at the touch of his hands. ''I'm not going to hurt you,'' he told her.

She tried to move away from him but he held her tightly.

''Please, Mr. Conrad,'' she said in a weak voice and turned her head to the side as if she were seeking some means of escape from him.

He drew her closer to him, so close that he could feel both the heat of her body and its trembling. He was reminded of a doe in the forest, one that scented danger riding in on the wind.

"I think you're a fine-looking woman, Miss Adams—Lorelei."

She shuddered as if his use of her given name had somehow unnerved her.

He bent down and tried to kiss her. She turned her head this way and that, evading his seeking lips. He reached up with one hand and cupped the back of her head, forcing her face toward his own. Their lips met. She hammered his chest with both fists. He was barely aware of the attack. Then, after a moment, she slowly relaxed and let him kiss her. As he drew away from her a moment later, she blinked up at him, seeming to become aware of where she was and what she had been doing.

"Mr. Conrad, *please!*"

Not really a request but a command which, though nonspecific, nevertheless made Gabe release her and step back.

"I didn't know you would try to exact a price for all the help you gave me tonight," Lorelei said, unable to meet Gabe's gaze.

He watched her standing there as she rubbed her arms where his hands had held her, wondering if tears were on the way to her. "Miss Adams, what I gave you, I gave freely. It had no price. I think you've got me wrong. What I was feeling for you, that had nothing to do with my lending you a hand so you could make a go of it as a teacher here at the school. I'm sorry you read me wrong. I guess the trouble with me is I'm still doing a lot of things the way the Lakota do them."

"I suppose that is something else you should have taught me. The Lakota men are rough and rude and

Lakota women are expected to be free with their favors."

"Once again you got it all wrong, Miss Adams. Wrong as a three-legged rooster, in fact. Lakota men aren't like you just described them but they are wide open to love and loving. So are Lakota women. Both Lakota men and women don't beat around the bush nearly as much as white folks do where sex is concerned. I'm sorry if I offended you. I didn't mean to and that's the truth. I only—well, I guess I'd better shut my mouth before I put my other foot in it."

Gabe turned and started for the door.

"Where are you going?" Lorelei called out to him.

"Well, it's clear I'm not going to get to spend the night here with you so I'll camp outside."

"There's no need of that. The agency has a guest house. It's two doors down. You can spend the night there."

"I suppose now you won't be going with me to Sitting Bull's camp come morning."

"I will if we can both manage to put what happened here just now behind us, Mr. Conrad. Can you do that?"

"I can, Miss Adams. But I wonder—now don't get me wrong, I don't mean to sound prideful when I ask you this. Can you put what happened, what nearly happened, between the two of us, behind you?"

Gabe didn't wait for Lorelei's answer. He opened the door and stepped outside into the cold December night.

As Gabe drove Lorelei's surrey, with his sorrel tied to its rear, into Sitting Bull's camp the following afternoon, he was greeted with enthusiastic cries in the Lakota language from the crowd that quickly gathered to welcome him.

"What are they saying?" a somewhat tense Lorelei asked him as she scanned the smiling faces surrounding them.

"Welcome back, Long Rider," he answered somewhat curtly.

"Long Rider?"

"It's what they call me." Gabe silenced any more questions by calling out a greeting to Sky Walking Woman and Hears Thunder as he drew rein in front of their tipi. He got out of the surrey and then, extending a hand, he helped Lorelei step down to the ground. "Miss Adams," he said, "I'd like to introduce you to Hears Thunder and his sister, Sky Walking Woman."

"How do you do?" Lorelei asked, managing a smile.

Sky Walking Woman merely stared intently at Lorelei.

Hears Thunder said, "How, *Kola*."

"Miss Adams came back with me to sit in on the Buffalo Sing which I figure we can hold tonight if everything's pretty much all set."

"I have gifts for the guests," Sky Walking Woman, suddenly smiling and animated, told Gabe. "I will make a stew for all of us. Warm Blanket is ready and terribly excited."

"We have built the ceremonial lodge while you were gone," Hears Thunder declared. "Also a purification lodge for you, Long Rider."

"I have dried chokecherries and I have gathered sage and sweetgrass," Sky Walking Woman announced, her eyes sparkling.

At that moment, Warm Blanket emerged from the tipi and stood looking everywhere but at Gabe.

"Take the woman's rig behind the lodge," Hears Thunder ordered her. "Then take Long Rider's and the woman's horses to the herd boy outside of camp."

Warm Blanket started to leave and then looked back at her mother. "Is it to be?" she asked shyly.

"Yes, my daughter," answered a smiling Sky Walking Woman. "Tonight we will hold the Buffalo Sing."

A smile flickered on Warm Blanket's face and then she leaped up into Lorelei's surrey and drove it around the tipi and out of sight.

"Would it be all right if Miss Adams uses Strong Heart's empty tipi until it's time for her to return to the agency tomorrow?" Gabe asked Hears Thunder, who answered, "No one will stop her."

"Sky Walking Woman, I would like to borrow blankets for Miss Adams," Gabe said. "She'll need them when night comes and it grows colder."

Sky Walking Woman, expressionless, looked from Gabe to Lorelei and then entered the tipi, returning a moment later with two blankets which she handed to Gabe.

"This way," Gabe said after thanking Sky Walking Woman for the blankets which he handed to Lorelei. He led her to Strong Heart's empty tipi, in which he and Sky Walking Woman had spent several sweet hours two nights earlier.

Once inside the shelter, he wordlessly proceeded to build a fire in the pit in the center of the ground.

"Hears Thunder—he was the man you rescued in town, wasn't he?"

"Hears Thunder and me, we met in town, yes."

Gabe fanned the fire and said, "This ought to keep you warm. I'll be right back."

"Where are you going?"

"Back to Hears Thunder's lodge. Sit down. Make yourself comfortable."

"On the ground?"

"On the ground. Sit on one of those blankets. If you're cold, wrap the other one around you."

Gabe turned and ducked under the entrance flap of the tipi. He made his way to Hears Thunder's lodge where he was about to use the bear-claw rattle hanging on it to announce his presence when Warm Blanket appeared from the rear of the lodge.

"Long Rider," she said and then fell silent.

"Don't be shy," he said to her. "If you've got something to say to me, you just go right ahead and say it. I'm listening."

"You have made my mother and my uncle very happy."

"I have?"

"They think it an honor to have you, Long Rider, perform the ceremony for me. You are not just a Buffalo Dreamer. You are also Long Rider. My mother says she will always remember my Buffalo Sing."

"I'm glad to do it, Warm Blanket, and that's the truth."

Warm Blanket ducked down and peered into the tipi. She said something Gabe couldn't hear and then her head reappeared. "My mother says you are to come in."

Long Rider entered the lodge and then so did Warm Blanket.

"I came to tell you—" he began, addressing Sky Walking Woman.

But Sky Walking Woman interrupted him. "Who is she? Why did you bring her here?"

"You mean Miss Adams? She's the teacher at the agency boarding school. As far as why did I bring her here, I brought her because she wants to learn all she can about the People so she'll be a better teacher. I invited her to come to the Buffalo Sing tonight."

Sky Walking Woman's features hardened but she said nothing.

Gabe turned to Warm Blanket. "Speaking of the boarding school, I wonder would you do something for me."

"Yes, I would. Gladly. What would you have me do?"

"Talk to the families in camp who have children. Tell them Long Rider said he thinks it wise for them to send their children to the white man's school at Standing Rock where they will learn many things that will be of value to them in the new time that is coming."

"I will do it," Warm Blanket said with a smile. And then she was gone.

"The People do not send their children to the agency school," Hears Thunder said, "because they fear the soldiers at Fort Yates."

"No soldier's going to shoot children," Gabe assured him. "And it's important that they learn what the white man—or, in this case, the white woman, Miss Adams—can teach them. They will need such knowledge in the future if the Lakota are to survive."

"They will lose their heritage in the agency boarding school," Sky Walking Woman said sharply. "That is what you want for them?"

"No, they won't and no, I don't," Gabe countered sharply. "They can keep their Lakota heritage while learning of the new world that is being forced upon the People. That is good. I have no more to say on this matter.''

Sky Walking Woman lowered her gaze and remained silent.

Gabe, quenching the fire of impatience that had suddenly flared within him, said in a lighter tone of voice, ''Let's not argue among ourselves. You know I would do nothing to harm the People.''

''I know that,'' Hears Thunder said firmly with a meaningful glance at his sister.

She drew a breath and then said, ''I, too, know that.''

Outside the tipi, a man shouted. A single word. *''Wasicu!''*

Gabe turned and went outside where he stood staring at the two riders entering the camp.

Indian Agent McLaughlin. And Sergeant Red Tomahawk of the reservation police.

Both drew rein in front of Gabe.

''Good day to you, Mr. Conrad,'' McLaughlin said.

Gabe nodded an acknowledgment of the greeting.

''Is Sitting Bull in camp?'' the agent inquired.

''Can't answer that,'' Gabe said, ''Haven't seen him since I got back here.''

''Well, I shall go to his lodge and see if he's there.''

''You're here to tell him to lay off the ghost dancing, I believe, based on what you told me yesterday at the agency.''

''Yes, that's correct. But, put another way, I'm here to head off any possible trouble that might develop between the Indians on this reservation and the military.''

''You think there's the likelihood of trouble, do you?'' Gabe pressed.

McLaughlin, smiling, wagged a playful finger at

Gabe. "Mind you, I did not say 'likelihood.' I said 'possible'."

"Do you have any objections to me sitting in on your meeting with Sitting Bull?" Gabe asked.

McLaughlin hesitated, but only briefly, before saying, "Of course not. Come along with the sergeant and myself. You may be able to do us some good, Mr. Conrad. That is to say, you may be able to help me persuade Chief Sitting Bull of the wisdom of the course I have come here to recommend once again to him and his people."

The trio made their way through the camp to Sitting Bull's tipi, followed by the eyes of a few Indians who stood watching them in silence. When they reached it, they found Sitting Bull standing in front of his lodge with his arms folded across his chest.

"I heard you had come here, McLaughlin," Sitting Bull said without preamble. "What is it you want this time?"

McLaughlin dismounted. "I want only the best for you, you know that, Chief."

Sergeant Red Tomahawk also dismounted and took McLaughlin's reins.

"Brrr," McLaughlin said, slapping his arms against his body. "It's a cold day, no two ways about that. Maybe we should talk inside. I can see by the smoke coming from your tipi that you have a fire going."

"We will talk here," Sitting Bull said, not moving. "Say what you have come to say to me."

"Well," McLaughlin said, looking at Red Tomahawk, at Gabe, at Sitting Bull again whose eyes were on the ground. "Well, to get down to it, I received your request to attend a Ghost Dance that you say is to be held at Chief Big Foot's camp on the Cheyenne River reservation. I hasten to tell you that I am heartily pleased to find that you are not planning any such events for Standing Rock. I am very glad we are not in dispute over that particular matter. However, I must explain my position to you.''

"It would be good of you to do that, McLaughlin," Gabe interjected. "Especially if you can do it without beating around a whole lot of bushes."

McLaughlin glared at Gabe, his face reddening. Then he turned his attention again to Sitting Bull and his face grew even redder as he became aware of the fact that the chief was smiling as a result of Gabe's remark.

"I have received instructions from Congress through Colonel Drum at Fort Yates that all such events are to be not only discouraged but outlawed. That means *any* Ghost Dance held on *any* of the four reservations in this part of the country."

"You are telling me I cannot go to Chief Big Foot's camp?" Sitting Bull asked through clenched teeth.

"No, I am not telling you that. I am telling you that you will not be permitted to go to Chief Big Foot's camp to attend or participate in a Ghost Dance," McLaughlin explained.

Sitting Bull, looking at Gabe, said, "The white men come and kill the buffalo so that our bodies starve. Now they try to kill our religion so that our spirits will also starve. At the same time, they, like this man here, tell us they are the Indian's friend. I grow old and maybe my mind is not as good as it once was. I cannot understand how men who say they mean the Indians well can do these things to us. Is it good in their eyes, do you think, to kill the Indians' bodies and their spirits?"

McLaughlin was about to say something but Gabe interrupted him. "What would you do, McLaughlin, if

Sitting Bull, backed up by some of his braves like you're backed up today by Red Tomahawk, stood in your church door tomorrow and kept you from attending Sunday services?''

"I see what you're getting at, Conrad."

Gabe noted the fact that he was no longer *Mr.* Conrad as far as Mclaughlin was concerned.

"We are not trying to stamp out a religion," the agent continued. "We are trying to prevent a revolution."

"That's nonsense and you know it," Gabe argued.

"What I know or don't know has nothing to do with the issue. I have my orders. I have my duty to perform. If Sitting Bull refuses to cooperate, refuses to listen to reason, I shall have to take punitive measures against him for the good of the majority of the Indian people."

"You're all of a sudden a spokesman for the majority of the Lakota, are you?" Gabe asked. "Since when and by whose decree?"

"I refuse to be drawn into a useless and, indeed, counterproductive argument on this subject," Mc-Laughlin said loudly, almost shouting now.

Sergeant Red Tomahawk stepped forward and spoke to Sitting Bull. "There are many soldiers at Fort Yates. They have many guns. Do not do this foolish thing. Do not leave the reservation for Big Foot's camp."

"I knew your mother," Sitting Bull said to the policeman. "A good woman. But she has borne a son of the wrong color. Why do you not paint your face white to match the color of your mind and heart, Red Tomahawk?"

Gabe saw the fury blaze in the sergeant's eyes. He saw the man's right hand drop to the butt of the gun he wore in a holster hanging from the cartridge belt that was strapped over his three-quarter length uniform coat.

"You are insulted by my words?" asked Sitting Bull in a calm voice. "Then make me swallow them. Leave the white man's camp and come to mine where you belong. We will welcome you with much joy as one would welcome the child who has strayed but returns to the place where he belongs."

"Enough of this!" McLaughlin snapped. "Sitting Bull, you are not to leave the reservation. I refuse to grant permission for you to travel to the Cheyenne River reservation. That is the end of it."

Gabe watched McLaughlin and the sergeant climb back aboard their horses, turn them, and start to ride out of the camp.

An uneasiness settled on him as Red Tomahawk glanced over his shoulder, and Gabe saw the anger burning in the Indian policeman's eyes as he stared fixedly at Sitting Bull.

CHAPTER SIX

"Tomorrow I go," Sitting Bull said stolidly when McLaughlin and Red Tomahawk had disappeared from sight.

"To Chief Big Foot's camp?" Gabe asked.

"Do you wish to come with me and the others who want to attend Bid Foot's Ghost Dance?"

"I do, yes. But I wonder if it might be better to wait until things settle down some before any of us go to any Ghost Dance."

"You are afraid, Long Rider?"

"You know better than to ask me that, Sitting Bull."

"It is hard for you, I know. You see with one eye on the white world and the other on the red world. It is not an easy way to live."

"I've got to tell you you're right about that."

"You have loved ones in the Land of Many Lodges. A wife. A mother. A father. If you dance, you may be able to go there to visit them."

The possibility of seeing his wife, Yellow Buckskin

Girl, again, along with his parents intrigued Gabe but part of him rejected the notion that such a thing was possible. What were these alleged visits by some of the dancers to the Land of Many Lodges he wondered. Trance states? Mesmerism? Self-induced hallucinations? He didn't know. He refused to reject out of hand the possibility that such things could happen. They had happened, he had heard, to Christian men and women of mystical bent. Would they happen to him?

"When do you plan to leave?" he asked Sitting Bull.

"Tomorrow before the sun rises but when there is light in the east."

"Do you plan to attend the Buffalo Sing tonight?"

"I do." Sitting Bull reached out and placed a hand on Gabe's shoulder. "I tell you this Long Rider. It is good to have you among us. It is good that you, a Buffalo Dreamer, will perform the Buffalo ceremony for a woman of the People. It lifts my spirit."

As Sitting Bull entered his tipi, Gabe turned and made his way back to Strong Heart's lodge. He pounded the flat of his hand on the hide covering and, when Lorelei called out, "Who is it?" he didn't answer but instead entered the tipi. He found Lorelei standing stiffly where he had left her, the two blankets Sky Walking Woman had given her on the ground by her feet.

"Has he gone?" she asked him.

"Who?"

"Mr. McLaughlin. I heard the commotion and looked out and saw him."

"You should have come out and said hello to him."

"I didn't want him to see me."

"Why not?"

"He might think it inappropriate for me to be here."

Gabe shook his head in puzzlement.

"A woman alone," Lorelei said, "one without a chaperone—"

"I have to go now. I just came to tell you I'll be back to get you and take you to the ceremony tonight."

"Must you leave me alone again?"

"I have to practice the purification rite before I perform the Buffalo Sing."

"I could come with you."

Gabe smiled to himself. "I don't think you'd want to. The purification rite—it means I strip till I'm buck naked and take what you might call a steam bath."

"Oh." A blush crimsoned Lorelei's face.

Gabe, still smiling, left her.

He went to where he had seen the ceremonial lodge and the sweat lodge Hears Thunder said had been constructed for his use.

The dome-shaped sweat lodge had been built of willow poles over which buffalo robes had been laid in such a manner as to make the structure virtually airtight. Its entrance, as was traditional, faced toward the east.

Outside the purification lodge, a shallow fire pit had been dug. Beside it on the ground were several large stones. Next to the stones rested a buffalo bladder filled with water together with a pipe and a pouch of tobacco.

Gabe hunkered down and proceeded to build a fire. When it was burning brightly, he placed several of the stones in it and then stripped his clothes from his body, shivering as he did so in the cold air. Using forked sticks, he carried four stones, once they had become hot, into the sweat lodge. He placed each of them in the indentation that had been made in the ground in the center of the lodge, then he retrieved the water pouch, pipe, and tobacco from outside.

He sat down on the sprays of sage that had been spread on the ground inside the lodge and proceeded to pack the pipe's bowl with tobacco and light it. He smoked, pointing the pipe in all four directions of the compass and to *Skan*, the sky. Then, singing a prayer, he sprinkled water from the buffalo pouch four times on the hot stones, from which hissing clouds of steam arose to drift throughout the sweat lodge.

He repeated the elements of the purification ritual several more times in the proper sets of four—the smoking of the pipe, the sprinkling of the stones with water, the singing of his prayers for purification.

He had no sense of time passing, only an awareness of the clouds of steam that filled the lodge. The thick vapor seemed to be about to smother him at times. The steam brought the sweat in a wet sheen to cover his lean body and it brought sought after visions to his receptive mind.

He saw a spider spinning. A turtle making its ponderous way across the land. A lark, singing. A brave man. Children. A smoking tipi.

The moist heat in the lodge gradually became intense. The steam swirled around Gabe, blinding him to all except his inner visions, which swirled, like the steam, in his mind. So intense did the heat become at one point that he was roused from his mind's journeying by pain in several places on his bare skin.

He promptly applied the traditional Lakota remedy for such superficial but nevertheless painful burns. He broke off a sprig from one of the sprays of sage covering the ground, chewed it to a pulp, and then applied it to his burns. The remedy worked; a welcome coolness came to the injured spots on his skin and their inflammation began to fade.

More time passed and then it was over. Gabe took a deep breath, wiped his body with sage until it was dry, then went outside to stand shivering in the cold darkness that had descended during the ritual, his body purified, his mind fortified with visions that would serve him well in the Buffalo Sing that lay ahead.

He dressed and went to Strong Heart's lodge. There he told Lorelei that it was time. "Are you hungry?" he asked her as they left the tipi together.

"Yes, I am."

"There'll be food at the ceremony. Sky Walking Woman will serve it afterward."

Gabe led Lorelei to the ceremonial lodge where they found a number of people gathered outside, Sitting Bull among them. There were others already seated inside the lodge they discovered as they entered it. Gabe directed Lorelei to a seat on a buffalo robe to the right of the entrance and then turned to Hears Thunder who was standing on the far side of the fire.

Hears Thunder bent down and picked up a skin cap which had buffalo horns at the side and a skin pendant hanging down the back. It was adorned with hawks' feathers on the cap, weasels' skins on the pendant, and the tail of a buffalo was attached to the lower end of the pendant.

Gabe put on the horned cap and then stripped to the waist. Using paint given him by Hears Thunder, he painted his face and body red and put three stripes of black paint across his face, from his right eye to his jaw, the red paint to indicate his spiritual power and the black stripes to indicate his authority to perform the Buffalo Sing.

"All is ready," Hears Thunder informed him.

Gabe glanced at the pipe, sweetgrass, wooden bowl,

dried chokecherries, eagle plume with its quill wrapped
with the skin from the head of a mallard drake, and
other items prepared for the ceremony, all of which
rested on a robe near the *catku*, the seat of honor, which
Hears Thunder, in the absence of Warm Blanket's deceased father, would occupy during the ceremony.
Halfway between the *catku* and the fire, a buffalo skull
sat on its altar, a raised mound of earth.

Gabe took his place to the left of the *catku*. He turned
and stood facing the door of the lodge opposite him,
the fire and buffalo skull between him and it.

As if responding to some prearranged signal, the
people gathered outside began to file into the lodge until every space around the tipi's perimeter was taken.
Those without seats remained outside, watching through
the open flap of the tipi.

Hears Thunder, at a nod from Gabe, took coals from
the fire burning in the center of the lodge and proceeded to light a spirit fire a few feet in front of the
catku.

While he was doing this, Gabe spread sage over the
catku and the space between it and the mound on which
the buffalo skull rested as well as around the fire to
keep evil spirits at bay. He lighted the pipe with the
spirit fire and blew some of its smoke into the nose
cavity and eye sockets of the buffalo skull before handing the pipe to Hears Thunder, who smoked and handed
it to the man next to him.

As the pipe passed slowly around the perimeter of
the lodge, Gabe took the bowl of red paint Hears Thunder handed him and painted the right side of the skull's
forehead down to the eye socket to show that his ceremony belonged to the Buffalo and that the girl for whom
it was to be performed would thereby become a buffalo

woman. He then stuck two wands he received from
Hears Thunder on the skull's mound so that they stood
within the curves of the skull's horns, each wand bearing a small package of medicine tied in red buckskin
to please the Spirit of the Buffalo and to let it know that
its spiritual essence contained in the medicines on the
wands was respected.

After sprinkling sweetgrass on the spirit fire to get the
attention of the supernatural powers, Gabe said, "My
friends, we have smoked with the Spirit of the Buffalo and
the spiritual essence of *Tatanka* will be with us in this
lodge." He followed his announcement with the traditional song called for at this point in the ceremony.

> Buffalo bull in the west, lowing.
> Buffalo bull in the west, lowing.
> Lowing, he speaks.

Then he laid a bit of red cloth on the skull as a
sacrifice, saying, "My older sister, I give this robe to
you." Turning, he said, "Bring to me now the girl who
would become a buffalo woman."

Moments later, Warm Blanket, eyes cast down, entered
the lodge, accompanied by her mother. Sky Walking
Woman seated Warm Blanket at the north side of the tipi,
Warm Blanket sitting cross-legged, as boys and men sit.

Gabe sprinkled more sage on the spirit fire and called
on several supernatural beings. "*Iya*, go away from this
place that this girl may not be a lazy woman." Sprinkling more sage on the spirit fire, he said, "*Iktomi*, go
away from this place that this girl may not do foolish
things." Again sprinkling sage on the fire, he said,
"*Anog Ite*, go away from this place that this girl may
not do shameful things when she is a woman." He

sprinkled the sage on the fire for the fourth time and said, "*Hochnogia*, go away from this place that this girl may not have trouble when she is a woman."

He waited then for the sage to stop smoking, aware of Lorelei Adams' eyes on him. When the smoke had dissipated, he sprinkled sweetgrass on the fire, saying, "*Tatanka*, I have painted your woman's forehead red and have given her a red robe. Her medicine is within her horns. Command her to give her spirit to this girl so that she may be a good buffalo woman and bear many children."

Turning to Warm Blanket, he said, "You are now a woman and should be ashamed to sit like a child. You should sit like a woman."

On cue, Sky Walking Woman rose and came over to Warm Blanket. She drew her daughter's limbs together at one side, after the manner of Lakota women.

Gabe, addressing Warm Blanket said, "You should always sit as you are now sitting." He walked around Warm Blanket four times before seating himself in front of her and saying, "I sought a vision in the purification lodge and I saw the messenger of the White Buffalo Cow. I sang this song:

The messenger of the buffalo in the West
The messenger of the buffalo in the West
The messenger of the buffalo in the West
I will give you a robe.

"Then the messenger said, 'A spider, a turtle, the voice of the lark, a brave man, children, a smoking tipi.' I will tell you what this means. The spider is industrious and builds a tipi for its children. It provides them with plenty of food. The turtle is wise and hears many

things but does not tell anything. Its skin is like a shield
so that arrows cannot wound it. The lark is cheerful
and brings the warm weather. It does not scold its people. It is always happy. If a brave man takes you for his
woman you may sing his scalp song and you may dance
his scalp dance. He will kill plenty of game so that you
will have skins and robes. You will bear him many children and he will make you happy. There will always be
a fire in your tipi and you will have food for your people. If you are industrious like the spider, wise like the
turtle, cheerful like the lark, then you will be chosen
by a brave man and have plenty and never be ashamed.

"I also saw these things in my vision: a coyote and
wornout moccasins. I heard a voice in mourning. The
Buffalo sends this message to you. If you listen to
Iktomi, or to *Iya*, or to *Anog Ite*, then you will be lazy
and poor and miserable. A brave man or a good hunter
will not give a dog for you. Your robes will be old and
ragged and your moccasins will be worn and without
color on them. The buffalo horns are on my head and
I speak in the spirit of the Buffalo. I am the buffalo
bull and you are a young buffalo cow. I will show you
what the evil spirits would have you do. I will show
you what the good spirits would have you do."

Gabe signaled to the drummers who began to drum
and to sing a song without words, some of the women
joining in their singing.

Gabe went to the south side of the lodge and began
to dance towards Warm Blanket, keeping time with the
drumming. As he danced, he uttered a guttural cry,
"Un-hu-hu-hu-ah," over and over again, continuing to
dance around Warm Blanket. He then got down on his
hands and knees near the door and bellowed like a buffalo bull. He caught a glimpse of Lorelei's startled ex-

pression as he began to paw the earth and throw it up in the manner of a rutting buffalo bull. Near her, Sitting Bull had a smile on his face. Gabe sniffed and then moved forward on his hands and knees toward Warm Blanket, blowing as buffalo bulls do when mating. He approached her on the right side, sidling up against her.

Sky Walking Woman hurried to her daughter and placed a bunch of sage under Warm Blanket's right arm so that it covered her right breast.

Gabe then approached Warm Blanket in the same way but on the left side.

Sky Walking Woman placed sage under her daughter's left arm to cover her left breast.

When he approached Warm Blanket from the front, Sky Walking Woman tossed sage into her daughter's lap.

He rose and returned to his seat at the right of the *catku*. Taking the wooden bowl and pouring water into it, he mixed chokecherries with the water while singing a wordless song. He then said to Warm Blanket, "We are buffalo on the plains. Here is a water hole. It is red to show that it belongs to the buffalo woman. Drink from it." He placed the bowl on the ground in front of Warm Blanket who drank from it.

Gabe then got down on his hands and knees, went to the bowl and also drank from it. Then, rising with the bowl in his hands, he said, "My friends, this girl gives you this red water that you may drink from it and be her friends. Let all who are her friends drink of it."

Gabe passed the bowl to Hears Thunder who drank from it and then passed it on. As the bowl passed from hand to hand, Gabe replenished the water and chokecherries as necessary and then gave Warm Blanket a piece of sage and told her to eat it.

"Sage is bitter," he told her as she chewed. "Your mother has shown you how it will keep away bad things." He then gave her a bit of sweetgrass and told her to eat it. While she was chewing it, he told her, "Sweetgrass is good. It pleases the Great Spirit and you should remember these things."

He took the wands from between the horns of the skull and, handing them to Warm Blanket, said, "This is your buffalo medicine. You should always keep it, for it will keep bad spirits away from you. It has the spirit of the Buffalo. It will keep *Anog Ite*, double-faced woman and goddess of shameful things, away from you. It will bring you many children."

He beckoned to Sky Walking Woman who stepped forward and arranged her daughter's hair in womanly fashion by parting it carefully across the top of the head and then braiding each half.

Gabe painted the right half of Warm Blanket's forehead red and ran a red streak across her head at the parting of her hair, saying as he did so, "You see your oldest sister on the altar. Her forehead is painted red. This is to show that she is divine. Your first flow was red. Then you were divine. You have taken red water this day. This is to show that you are akin to *Tatanka*, the Buffalo, and his woman. *Tatanka* is pleased with an industrious woman. He is pleased with a woman who gives food to those who are hungry. He will make brave men desire her so they will pay a large price for her. She may choose the man she desires. If he has other wives, it is she who will sit next to the *catku*. They will carry wood while she makes moccasins. You are now a buffalo woman, Warm Blanket. You may paint your face this way."

Gabe tied the eagle plume to Warm Blanket's hair at

the top of her head, saying as he did so, "The spirit of the eagle and the duck will be with you. They will give you many children."

As he began to chant a song without words, Warm Blanket turned and left the ceremonial lodge, followed by her mother, her uncle, and then all the invited guests. When they had all gone, Gabe leveled the mound of earth that had supported the buffalo skull so that it might not be desecrated.

He overturned the buffalo skull so that its horns touched the ground to symbolize a buffalo resting on the ground at night, thus giving rest to the skull's spirit. Then he divested himself of his buffalo-horned skin cap and washed the paint from his face and body. After dressing, he left the lodge and went outside where he found Lorelei Adams waiting for him.

"You look like quite a different man," she said. "In the tipi—at times during the ceremony I hardly recognized you. You seemed to become a different person. You even looked different."

"The paint," he said.

"No, it was more than that. Of course, the paint did have something to do with your—your transformation. That seems to be the only word that truly fits. You were transformed before my very eyes into someone else. Someone I didn't know."

"Someone you were afraid of?"

Lorelei thought about the question for a moment and then nodded. "Yes, someone I was afraid of."

"No need to be afraid. Not of me." He paused a moment and then, "Let's go to Hears Thunder's lodge. There will be food there. We'll eat."

"I can hardly wait. I'm famished."

As they walked together through the camp, Gabe asked, "What did you think of the ceremony?"

"I found it altogether fascinating. Of course, there were things about it that I didn't fully understand. But, taken as a whole, I was quite impressed—if a little embarrassed."

"Embarrassed?" Gabe glanced at Lorelei, not understanding what she meant.

"Well, you'll have to admit it was a bit bold at times—you were."

"I don't think I follow you."

"Your playacting the part of the buffalo bull to Warm Blanket's cow. It was really quite explicit in its symbolic significance and highly erotic for such a public ceremony."

"But that's what the whole thing, at bottom, was all about. Warm Blanket becoming a woman, I mean, and learning about womanly things. Sex being one of them."

"And to speak publicly about her—I believe you referred to it as her 'flow'. I must confess I found that rather shocking."

Gabe was surprised—almost amazed—to see Lorelei blush and lower her gaze. "I understand now," he said. "I tend to forget that the People do things a lot different than the way whites do them—or don't do them, I guess would be the proper way to put it. There's nothing to be embarrassed about when somebody speaks of the natural way of things. The ceremony celebrated Warm Blanket's first menses. It made her a buffalo woman. She was taught what a woman of the Lakota people should do and be. You might as well be embarrassed about teaching sums and spelling to your scholars at the agency."

"That's not the same thing."

"Sure it is. It's all part of what's real in the world. Here we are."

Gabe held the tipi flap aside so Lorelei could enter Hears Thunder's lodge which was crowded with talking, laughing people, all of them with wooden bowls of steaming stew in their hands.

He led Lorelei to the right and found them an empty spot. They were barely seated when Sky Walking Woman appeared before them, two large bowls in her hands. She gave one to Gabe, the other to Lorelei.

Lorelei looked at the large sodden lump in her bowl and then at Gabe. "What is this?" she whispered.

Sky Walking Woman smiled as Gabe answered, "Puppy-dog stew. That's the puppy's head you've got there. It's considered the choicest part and usually goes to an honored guest."

"Eat," Sky Walking Woman said to Lorelei.

Gabe fished with his fingers in his bowl and came up with part of a hind leg which he began to gnaw on.

Lorelei stared at him, transfixed, her bowl cradled in her hands, its contents untouched. She continued to stare at him as he tore the flesh from the dog's leg and chewed it, grease staining his lips and chin as he did so. Then she looked down again at the puppy's head that floated in the broth in her bowl. She quickly put down the bowl, jumped to her feet and, with both hands covering her mouth, fled from the tipi.

Sky Walking Woman's laughter followed her outside. So did Gabe. "You should have *pretended* to eat at least," he said to her angrily. "You insulted Sky Walking Woman."

"I think I'm going to be sick," Lorelei moaned, clutching her stomach.

"Take a deep breath. Now, another." When Lorelei had done so, Gabe asked, "Feel any better?"

"Some, yes. Thank you."

"You want to go back inside and try again to down some of that—"

"No!" Lorelei's cry was more of a lament than it was a refusal. Tears began to leak from her eyes as she stood facing Gabe.

"What's wrong?"

"Everything. I shouldn't have come here. First, I had to witness that disgusting display you put on and then I was offered *dog* to eat!"

"Maybe you're right. Maybe you shouldn't have come here. The Lakota way isn't your way. Trying to get to know it, to understand it—well, maybe it's true that it's best to leave well enough alone."

"I wanted to get to know the Lakota culture. I didn't want to be embarrassed and disgusted by it."

Gabe shrugged noncommittally.

"You think I'm awful, don't you?"

"I think you just got a bit more than you bargained for tonight. I shouldn't have brought you here."

"But I wanted to come. It's not your fault. It's all mine. Oh, I feel so awful. So ashamed of myself for being such a ninny!"

"I'll tell you something. My mother was taken captive by the Lakota, which is how I came to be raised as one of them. When I got old enough to understand, my mother told me about how hard it was for her when she first came to live among the People. There were times, she told me, when she wanted to die. Everything, she said, was so different from what she had been used to. Some of it she found disgusting, the same as you did tonight. But by the time she got to know the

Lakota better, she said, she found out that they were, most of them, good people. Kind and generous and ready to help out when somebody needed help. She got so she could see the good things about the Lakota way of life.

"Tonight—this was your first plunge into it all. Maybe it was too much too fast. Or maybe I should have told you what to expect. Don't take it so hard. It's not the end of the world."

Gabe reached out and placed his hands on Lorelei's shoulders. When she looked tearfully up at him, he said softly, "You wait here. I'll be right back." He left her standing under the round white eye of the full moon and returned to Hears Thunder's tipi. When he emerged from it several minutes later, he took Lorelei by the hand and led her to Strong Heart's empty tipi where he built a fire and then showed her the contents of his fur coat's pockets.

"Pemmican," he said. "Parched corn. It's not a feast, not by a long shot, but it ought to take the edge off your hunger and hold you until you can get back to the agency and have something better to eat."

"Pemmican?"

"It's dried lean meat mixed with some fat and pounded into little cakes. Try some. It's good. You'll like it."

Lorelei took the pemmican Gabe offered her and tasted it. "It is good. Where did you get it?"

"From Sky Walking Woman."

Lorelei sampled the corn and then ate some more of the pemmican. "I should go to Sky Walking Woman and apologize to her and to Warm Blanket for my offensive behavior."

"No need. I told her you were sorry. I explained that

you hadn't meant to insult her, that it was just that
you're eating habits didn't match those practiced by the
Lakota.''

''Thank you.'' Lorelei paused in her eating. ''I don't
think she likes me.''

''Who? Sky Walking Woman?''

''I think she resents the fact that you brought me here
to see the ceremony.''

''I find that hard to believe. She's a very friendly
person.''

''I may be wrong but I don't think I am. Call it a
matter of a woman's intuition. I saw the way she looked
at you and then looked at me when we first arrived. It
was as if she was about to melt when she looked at you
but she looked daggers at me. Is there something between you two?''

Gabe was taken aback by the question. He considered his answer for several moments before replying,
''Just friends is all we are.'' Well, he told himself that
was true. They weren't lovers. Not after one brief encounter here in this very lodge. There was no commitment. Neither of them had any obligation to the other.

''Will Warm Blanket get married now that she is a
woman?'' Lorelei inquired.

''If a man desires her and pays a decent bride price
for her and she desires him, yes.''

''I envy her.''

Gabe said nothing, watching Lorelei who was staring
dreamily into the fire.

''She is young and free and has her whole life ahead
of her,'' Lorelei mused. She glanced at Gabe. ''You
have made her a woman. I'm sure she is very pleased.''

''The spirit of the Buffalo has made her a woman,''

Gabe said. "I was just what you might call the go-between."

"I think I knew from the moment I first saw you that you could make any woman feel truly womanly."

Gabe gave Lorelei a wry smile. "You're wrong about that. I seem to recall that nothing like that happened where you were concerned."

Lorelei hesitated a moment before saying anything more as if she were carefully considering her response. Then, "You're wrong, Mr. Conrad. What I did—or, rather what I didn't do that night in my lodgings when we were alone together—that had nothing to do with what I was feeling."

Gabe felt desire stir within him, a strong desire to possess Lorelei that he had carefully suppressed since the incident she had just referred to.

She was staring intently into his eyes now and for once it did not strike him as impolite for a person to do so. He matched her stare for a moment and then reached out and took her in his arms, fully expecting her to pull back, express shock, or get up and run out into the night.

She did none of those things. Instead, she kissed him squarely on the lips.

The desire stirring within him burst into full fiery life. He crushed her against him, returning her kiss with a passion that surpassed her own.

Their lips remained locked together as Gabe's hands began to explore her body, slipping under her heavy coat in order to do so better.

She moaned and pressed herself against him. Her hand touched his groin, squeezed his stone-stiff shaft, and was gone. He seized it and returned it to where his erection throbbed hotly, encouraging her to continue to caress it.

"Make me a woman, too, as you did Warm Blanket," Lorelei murmured in his ear. "Do it *now*."

And do it Gabe did.

They eagerly coupled after fumbling out of their clothes. Lying on one of the blankets Sky Walking Woman had given Lorelei, the heat of their passion matched that of the flames leaping up from the fire in the center of the tipi.

Gabe eased himself inside Lorelei, who received him with a grunt and an embrace. He slid back and forth, reveling in her wetness, delighting in the sensations that were coursing through him as Lorelei thrust her hips up against his and tossed her head from side to side, whispering words he could barely hear, but he was almost sure, at one point, he heard her mutter: *"Buffalo bull."*

She cried out his name—not Mr. Conrad, but Gabe—as she climaxed and her body convulsed, shivering with pleasure beneath him.

He kept up his steady pounding rhythm, letting himself go now that he had succeeded in giving her pleasure. His climax, when it came, was an explosive experience, one that made him cry out with pleasure and bury himself deep within Lorelei.

CHAPTER SEVEN

Early the next morning, Gabe went and got Lorelei's surrey ready and brought it to where she stood waiting for him in front of Strong Heart's lodge.

"What is going on?" she asked him, indicating the bustle of activity in the camp. "Why all the commotion?"

"Sitting Bull and some of his people are heading south to attend a Ghost Dance at Chief Big Foot's camp on the Cheyenne River reservation."

Lorelei frowned. "I thought the Ghost Dance was forbidden. Mr. McLaughlin told me when I arrived and asked him about all the rumors surrounding the Ghost Dance that it had been outlawed and the Indians were prohibited from practicing it."

"That's true enough," Gabe said, a definite sense of unease settling upon him. "But saying to someone you daren't do this is one thing. Stopping him from doing it, that's another."

"Will there be trouble?"

"I hope not."

"Are you going with the others? To the Ghost Dance?"

"I am."

"Forgive me if I sound foolish, Gabe, but I would prefer that you not go. I know it is none of my business. But I don't want to see you involved in what is clearly a dangerous situation, given the fact that the country seems to be swarming with soldiers."

"I thank you kindly for your sentiments, Lorelei. I like having someone care about what happens to me."

"I do care." Lorelei paused. "Will I see you again?"

Here it is, Gabe thought. It always comes down to this. What kind of an answer can I give her? The truth. Hell, I don't know what the truth is as it applies to her kind of question. How can a man like me who roams like the wind know where he will go or what he will do in the next five minutes, never mind a day or two down the road?

"I hope I get to see you again," he told Lorelei sincerely, knowing well it was not the answer she had hoped to hear.

"Well, that is something, I suppose," she said softly. "You could have told me you were off to Timbuktu, never to visit this part of the world again." She held out her hand to him.

He didn't take it. Instead, he took her in his arms and kissed her, causing several passing women to giggle and point at the pair.

"Long Rider."

Gabe let go of Lorelei and turned to find Warm Blanket standing behind him. "What is it?" he asked her.

"Yesterday, before the Buffalo Sing, I did as you

asked me to do. Nine children will go to the boarding school at the agency.''

Gabe suddenly remembered having asked Warm Blanket to tell the families with children in the camp that he thought it would be wise for them to send their children to Lorelei's school at Standing Rock. ''That's real good news, Warm Blanket. I thank you kindly for delivering my message.''

''What is all this?'' Lorelei asked. ''Is Warm Blanket saying—''

Gabe quickly explained that she would soon have nine more pupils.

''Oh, that's wonderful! I'm so pleased. Thank you ever so much, Gabe. Thank you too, Warm Blanket. Tell the families that I will send a wagon for the children just as soon as I get back to the agency.''

When Warm Blanket had gone, Gabe helped Lorelei up into the surrey's seat and then handed her the reins. ''You take good care of yourself, hear?''

She gave him a smile that had a touch of sadness in it before slapping the rump of her horse with the reins.

Gabe stood there, watching the surrey make its way across the flatland in the distance until it dwindled to a tiny black dot and finally disappeared from sight. He turned then and made his way to Hears Thunder's lodge.

When he got there, he found Hears Thunder, Sky Walking Woman, and Warm Blanket waiting for him and ready to leave.

''I will get your horse, Long Rider,'' Warm Blanket said and went running around the tipi.

''You're sure you want to do this thing?'' Gabe asked, his eyes drifting from Hears Thunder to Sky Walking Woman and back again. ''There may be danger.''

"Yes, the soldiers," Hears Thunder said and spat on the ground.

"Not just the soldiers," Gabe said. "There's Agent McLaughlin to consider as well. Him and his Indian police. They might take a notion, if they hear that Sitting Bull and some of his people have left the reservation, to light out after us."

"We will go," Sky Walking Woman said firmly. "We will dance," she added, her eyes brightening and her features relaxing into a soft smile. "I hope to dance my way to the Land of Many Lodges to visit my husband, White Eagle."

Before Gabe could say anything more, Warm Blanket came up to them at a run, leading Gabe's sorrel, on which she had placed his gear, and Hears Thunder's horse.

"Looks like we're all set," Gabe commented, looking around at the other people in camp who had already begun to leave the village.

"Not yet," Hears Thunder said and ducked under the tipi's entrance flap. When he returned, he carried a Henry rifle with a broken stock, which he handed to his sister.

Gabe watched in silence as Sky Walking Woman wrapped the loaded weapon in a blanket and gave it to her daughter to carry. Then the four of them joined the throng leaving the village and heading south.

There was an uproar in Chief Big Foot's Miniconjou Sioux camp when Gabe and the others in Sitting Bull's band arrived.

Old friends ran to greet and embrace one another. There were shouts of welcome, cries of joy, happy laughter, a few sentimental tears.

Dogs ran about and barked.

Babies cried.

Tipis went up as everyone pitched in to help the new-comers. Cooking fires were lit and food was shared.

Sitting Bull moved through what amounted to a jovial melee, saying little, seeing everything. When he was satisfied that the long one hundred-mile journey had been completed satisfactorily, he went over to where Gabe was helping Hears Thunder stretch a hide covering over their tipi poles.

"I go now to meet Chief Big Foot," Sitting Bull announced. "Will Long Rider come with me?"

"I'll come."

Sitting Bull asked a woman passing by for the location of the chief's camp and moments later he was thumping a callused hand on the hide covering of Big Foot's tipi that bore on it brightly painted scenes of Indians battling blue-coated soldiers.

A woman came out of the tipi and held the tipi's entrance flap aside so that Sitting Bull and Gabe could enter the shelter where a low fire burned.

Big Foot, inclining against a pile of buffalo robes with his legs stretched out in front of him, raised a hand in greeting.

"We have come to you," Sitting Bull said, "so that we may dance with you."

"I am glad my brother from the Hunkpapa council fire has come," Big Foot replied politely. "We will dance together, you and I." The Chief paused. "Who is this you bring with you, Sitting Bull?" he asked, not looking at Gabe.

"I bring you Long Rider of the Oglala Sioux," Sitting Bull replied with a sweep of his arm in Gabe's direction.

"Long Rider," Big Foot repeated. "Then the legend is true."

"It is true," Sitting Bull assured Big Foot. "This man is the legend. This is Long Rider."

"I have heard many men speak of you and your exploits," Big Foot said to Gabe. "They have spoken well. You are welcome to sit here by my fire, you and Sitting Bull."

Gabe and Sitting Bull sat down and then, after Big Foot had lighted his pipe, the three men passed it from hand to hand, smoking in silence for some time. When at last, the pipe's tobacco had been consumed, it was Big Foot who spoke first.

"Have you seen soldiers on your journey here?" he inquired.

"We saw some," Sitting Bull replied and added with a smile, "We saw to it that they did not see us."

Big Foot raised an eyebrow. "I take it then that Agent McLaughlin did not give his blessing to your journey here."

"He did not."

"I am not surprised. The whites fear us because we dance. Long Rider, did you come here to dance with us?"

Gabe wasn't sure how to reply. Had he come to participate in the Ghost Dance? Or had he come merely to witness it?

"You do not answer, Long Rider," Big Foot persisted. "Perhaps that is because you fear the dance as do your white brothers."

"I do not fear it," Gabe answered firmly. "I know little or nothing about it except what I have heard and what I have heard are whispers on the wind which may or may not be true. When I learned that Sitting Bull was coming here to your Ghost Dance, I decided to come along and learn all I could about it.''

"Would that other white men were as wise," Big Foot mused, folding his thin hands across his chest. ''Would that they would come to us and learn before they harshly judge what they do not understand and do not wish to understand. Such is the case with the pony soldiers. They are a thorn in our side here on the reservation. They are a bitter medicine we do not want to take.''

"They have given you trouble, Chief?" Gabe asked.

''They come to this camp from time to time to tell us what we must not do and what we must do. But they never come with food for my people, who are hungry. One day soon I will go to agency headquarters. There I will tell the agent to feed us or we shall die. It is a shameful thing I will do but do it I will unless the beef ration comes—and comes in time.''

Sitting Bull rose and asked, "When shall we dance?"

''There are others coming,'' Big Foot declared. ''Some from Pine Ridge. Some from Rosebud reservation. They have sent runners to tell me they will be here tomorrow. When they come, we will dance. When the sun rises two days from now.''

Gabe followed Sitting Bull from the tipi.

''I go now,'' Sitting Bull told him. ''My wives will have set up my tipi by now. I will rest as an old man must in the middle of the day. But you, Long Rider, you are a young man. Perhaps you will find a woman here in camp who will keep you company until it is time for us to dance.''

Gabe's grin matched the one wreathing Sitting Bull's face as he left the older man and made his way back to the tipi he was to share with Hears Thunder, Sky Walking Woman, and Warm Blanket.

When he arrived, he found only Sky Walking Woman there. She sat outside, a blanket wrapped tightly around her, and stirred a pot containing a steaming stew which hung above a cooking fire.

He sat down crosslegged on the ground beside her.

"Do you miss her?" Sky Walking Woman asked, gazing at her stew.

"Miss Adams?" Gabe glanced at Sky Walking Woman whose face bore no readable expression. "No, I don't miss her."

"You spent the night with her in Strong Heart's lodge."

An accusation? That's what Sky Walking Woman's observation sounded like to Gabe.

"I spent the night with you in the same lodge," he reminded her, avoiding any comment about Lorelei.

"But she is white."

So that's how the land lies, Gabe thought. Lorelei was right. Sky Walking Woman's jealous of her. Leave it to a woman to spot the kind of things most men, me included, would miss by a country mile.

"You will have her for your woman?"

"No. I don't plan on having any woman for a wife." Before Sky Walking Woman could say anything more, could take the conversation where Gabe did not want it to go, he got up and walked away, uncomfortably aware of her eyes boring into his back.

He spent an hour walking about the camp, stopping for a time to lend a hand to a crippled man who was having trouble digging a fire pit.

By the time he returned to his tipi, Sky Walking Woman was nowhere in sight, nor were Warm Blanket

or Hears Thunder. When he shook the bear-claw rattle
hanging on the tipi, Sky Walking Woman called out to
him to enter.

Inside the shelter, he found her standing with her
back to him. He was about to speak to her when she
turned, her arms spread wide, a buckskin garment displayed in both of her hands.

He knew it immediately for what it was: a ghost shirt.
It bore a painted sun, yellow as gold, and a buffalo with
vermilion blood on its horns. On the seams of the shirt's
three-quarter length sleeves were stitched several crow's
feathers, black as midnight.

"For you to wear in the Ghost Dance," Sky Walking
Woman said. "This ghost shirt was White Eagle's. It
will protect you from the white man's bullets."

"I appreciate it, Sky Walking Woman," Gabe said
sincerely. "But I'm not expecting any white man's bullets to come my way."

"But if they do, this shirt will keep you safe from
them."

Gabe was wearing the ghost shirt Sky Walking
Woman had given him two days later, his fur coat and
guns left behind in the tipi, as he and most of the others
in the Miniconjou camp gathered under the orange eye
of the rising sun and waited for the Ghost Dance to
begin.

In his hair he wore a feather that had been painted
blue in accordance with the advice given him the day
before by one of the seven priests who would conduct
the dance. It was tipped with a small down feather that
he had painted yellow, again on the advice of the priest
who had danced before and been granted a vision dur-

ing which he had learned about the proper dress and
ornamentation to be worn by the dancers.

He was now about to have his face painted and was
following the protocol for such a ritual, which he had
learned the day before from Hears Thunder.

He went up to the priest who had taught him how to
paint his feathers and, placing his hands upon the man's
head, said, "My father, I have come to be painted so that
I may see my friends. Have pity on me and paint me."

The priest, in wordless response to his plea, proceeded to paint an elaborate design in red, yellow, and
blue upon Gabe's face which consisted of several stars,
a cross, a crescent, and a crow. He concluded the ritual
by painting a yellow line along the part in Gabe's hair.

When all the dancers were ornamented, adorned, and
painted, the seven priestly leaders of the dance, stepped
out onto the open space at the edge of the camp that
was to be the dance ground, all of them facing inward
to form a small circle as they began to sing the opening
song of the dance.

While the song was being sung, all the dancers, Gabe
among them, stood motionless with their hands
stretched out toward the west, the country of the messiah and the place from which the new spirit world was
to come.

> The father says so—*E'yayo*!
> You shall see your grandfather—*E'yayo*!
> The father says so.
> You shall see your kindred—*E'yayo*!
> The father says so.

Gabe thought of Yellow Buckskin Girl. He thought
of his parents as the singing continued. When it ended,

he shouted with all the others, after which they all joined hands—not clasped in the white way, but with their fingers intertwined with those on either side of them in the way of the Ghost Dance—and began to circle around to the left. He matched the simple step of the other dancers—advancing the left foot and following it with the right, barely lifting the feet from the ground as another song was sung:

It is your father coming; it is your father coming,
A spotted eagle is coming for you,
A spotted eagle is coming for you.

Out of the corner of his eye, Gabe, as he danced with the crowd of men, women, and even small children, saw one of the seven priests pass Sitting Bull, Big Foot at his side, and move closer to him, an eagle feather that had been painted red held in his upraised hand.

The priest waved the feather in front of the eyes of each dancer as he came face-to-face with that person. Gabe turned his head as a woman to his left cried out. He saw her stiffen, saw her head tilt back, saw her eyes roll up into her head, saw her crumple to the ground.

The dancers stepped nimbly around her, closing the dance circle and allowing her to lie where she had fallen. So that's the way you get to the Land of Many Lodges, he thought. That's the "dying" in the dance I've heard talked about. He danced on, the words of the songs being sung, without accompaniment by any kind of instrument, not even a drum, a pounding rhythm in his ears and in his mind as well.

Suddenly, his eyes, which had begun to close, snapped wide open as the priest he had seen a moment ago materialized directly in front of him, waving the painted eagle feather he held in his hand.

As he moved it up and down before Gabe's eyes, he issued a steady series of sharp exclamations: *"Hu! Hu! Hu!,"* sounding to Gabe as he did so like an exhausted runner. The priest abruptly changed the direction of the feather, whirling it about now in a circle before Gabe's eyes, moving in time with the dancers, but keeping the feather moving in front of Gabe's face as he did so.

"Hu! Hu! Hu!"

The feather became a red blur before Gabe's eyes. The words of the song resounded hypnotically in his mind. The song, the singers, the rhythm of many feet, the priest's red feather moving this way then that before his eyes, circling, blazing . . .

"Hu! Hu! Hu! Hu!"

She was suddenly there before him, walking through a summery land, a basketful of huckleberries tucked under one brown arm.

Yellow Buckskin Girl, his deceased wife.

He knew at once that he was now in the Land of Many Lodges.

Smiling, with arms outstretched, he began to run toward her as around him a soft breeze blew and unseen birds sang in the shin oak trees.

She dropped her basket, sending huckleberries scattering in the long grass, and then she was running toward Gabe.

Their meeting was one that blended laughter and tears, shouts of joys and loud laments. They held each other close, turning, turning beneath the hot sun, speaking each other's name like a marvelous litany of love.

Then, holding Yellow Buckskin Girl out in front of

him at arm's length, Gabe said, "I've missed you more than I can ever say."

"I have missed you too, Long Rider. Through all the sad days and the empty nights, I have called your name as I longed to see you again."

"Now I am here and we are together."

She took his arm as they walked through a meadow full of wildflowers which displayed every color known to Gabe and some colors he had never seen before and could not name.

They chose a shady spot beneath the tallest of the shin oaks. There they sat and there they talked of times past and of days made bright by their togetherness and of nights made joyous by their lovemaking.

Later, they walked through a land that had the bluest sky Gabe had ever seen as well as the greenest grass, both of them almost blinding in their beauty. Yellow Buckskin Girl held Gabe's hand and, when he blurted out the fact that he wanted to stay and never leave her, she put a finger to his lips and shook her head.

"It is not yet time," she admonished him gently. "One day—but not this day, not today."

He knew she was right and damned the knowing. But all in the fullness of time, he told himself. She would be here waiting for him when the day came for him to walk the Spirit Trail in the sky. And walk it he would, he vowed, with a quick step and a head held high as he journeyed to join her so that they might share *Wakan Tanka's* gift of eternity together.

When he felt her hand withdraw from his, he turned to face her. Saw her take a step backward. Saw her smile dissolve into an expression of solemnity. Heard her whisper: "I love you." Heard himself call her name as she began to fade as her smile had just done. In moments, she was gone, leaving behind her only the sunlight on the green grass and a Gabe Conrad whose heart was breaking for the second time in his life in the face of a loss he believed he could not endure . . .

Cold. Cloudy.

Where?

He shuddered. Blinked. Heard the shouting, heard the sound of pounding hooves . . .

Saw clouds of dust rising and the Ghost Dancers running in every direction, some of the women shrieking, some of the men turning back to stand their ground, their ghost shirts brazenly displayed to the mounted soldiers who were galloping through the camp toward them.

Gabe struggled to his feet in the midst of the confusion and shouting, realizing that he, like the women he had seen earlier during the Ghost Dance, must have gone into a trance and lost consciousness.

That red feather in the hand of the priest, he thought, registered in his mind as a series of striking images. That's what did it.

Cavalry troopers riding in two long lines, successfully flanked the dancers and prevented them from fleeing to the nearby woods and then, closing ranks in the distance, completely bottled up the dancers.

Sitting Bull and Big Foot, stood tall and silent in the middle of the melee.

A colonel sat astride a big buckskin and surveyed the scene with a satisfied expression on his face, his polished boots glinting in the sunlight.

As Gabe looked around him, the colonel spurred his horse and rode slowly in the direction of Sitting Bull and Big Foot, who were still standing like two unarmed soldiers in the face of an overpowering enemy.

Gabe moved through the crowd toward the pair, his teeth set, the result of the tension he was feeling and, yes, he admitted it to himself, the fear he was feeling.

He arrived in time to hear the colonel say to Big Foot, "You know who I am."

"I know," Big Foot answered. "You are Colonel Sumner."

"Of the Eighth Cavalry. Do you also know why I have come here today?"

"To make trouble for us," Big Foot said.

"You may call it that if you wish," Sumner said with a prissy twitch of his blond mustache. "Actually, I was ordered to come here to keep the peace, which I fully intend to do."

"We are not making war," Big Foot pointed out.

"You are dancing again, Chief. I call that a prelude to war. A fine enough distinction but there you are."

"Who sent you?" Sitting Bull asked.

"Colonel Miles," Sumner answered. "When your absence from Standing Rock was discovered and reported to Agent McLaughlin, he contacted Colonel Miles who, as you no doubt know, is in charge of military activities here in Sioux country, for instructions as to what he should do. He was told to contact me to put down the uprising and I have come with my men to do just that."

"Colonel, is that what you saw happening here?" Gabe asked in a tight tone. "An uprising?"

Sumner gave him a quizzical glance. "And you, sir. "Who are you?"

"Name's Gabe Conrad. I'd appreciate an answer to my question."

"What are you doing here, Conrad, in the midst of all this?"

"Dancing."

"You? A white man? Dancing with these—these savages?"

"I answered your question and it seems like your ears are good enough to have heard what I said. Now, what I want to know is what uprising were you fixing to put down?"

"I apparently had the good fortune to arrive in time to prevent one from occurring," Sumner declared.

Gabe was about to say something more when, out of the corner of his eye, he saw Sky Walking Woman making her way through the crowd toward Hears Thunder in the distance. In her hands was a blanket which Gabe recognized as the one in which she had wrapped the Henry rifle her brother had given her before leaving the Standing Rock reservation.

The troopers, all of them watching the confrontation between Sumner on the one hand, and Sitting Bull, Big Foot and Gabe on the other, paid no attention to her.

Gabe, just before she reached Hears Thunder, went sprinting toward them. He arrived just as Sky Walking Woman unwrapped the rifle and handed it to her brother.

"Ready!" he heard Colonel Sumner call out from behind him.

"Take aim!"

Before Sumner could give the order to fire, Gabe ripped the rifle from Hears Thunder's hands and, turning so that Sumner would be sure to see him, he gripped it by the barrel in both hands and swung it high above his head, bringing it down to smash against the ground. Then, carrying the pieces of the broken weapon, he returned to Sumner.

The two men's eyes met.

"This, Colonel," Gabe said, "is the extent of your uprising. One rifle which, if fired, I'd wager would blow up in a man's face. Did you think you could have put down this so-called uprising by shooting the man with the gun? Maybe the woman who gave it to him, too? Is that what you call smart military tactics?"

"I resent your cavalier tone, Conrad," Sumner snapped. "But I must grudgingly commend you for disarming that savage." He shifted position in his saddle, his hands clasping his saddle horn as he stared down at Sitting Bull and Big Foot.

He didn't dismount, Gabe thought, so's he could sit up there above everybody else just like God. So's he could make the rest of us look up to him.

"By command of Colonel Nelson Miles, I hereby order you, Sitting Bull, to pack up your belongings, you and your people, and return post haste to Standing Rock. I will provide a military escort to see that you do as you have been ordered to do.

"As for you, Big Foot, you are ordered to hold no more so-called Ghost Dances. Not now. Not ever again. Is that understood?"

"I understand that the white man's fear steals our messiah from us and keeps us from visiting our friends and relatives at the end of the Spirit Trail."

Sumner muttered an expletive. "Enough of this nonsense," he bellowed. "I want a straight answer. Do you understand that henceforth there is to be no more fol-de-rol of this nature?"

Big Foot deigned to nod.

"Sitting Bull?" Sumner prompted.

The chief turned and called out to his people. "We go home." The two men walked away, turning their backs on Sumner.

Sumner turned his attention to Gabe. "I still don't know what you are doing here, sir. But let me give you a word of advice, if I may. Separate yourself from these people. There are storm clouds gathering on the horizon. Trouble lies ahead. But it is not your trouble. It is the Indians'."

"I cannot separate myself from these people," Gabe replied. "A man might separate himself from his heart but if he does, he dies." He turned on his heels and stalked away, following Sitting Bull and Big Foot, the other ghost dancers in turn following him.

CHAPTER EIGHT

The long after midnight return to Sitting Bull's camp was far different from the arrival in Big Foot's camp on the Cheyenne River. This time no friends or relatives ran to greet the people returning. Instead, when those who had remained in camp saw the soldiers, they either stood in stony silence watching their arrival or surreptitiously fled from the camp.

Gabe, still wearing his ghost shirt under his fur coat, was not wearing his sidearm, nor was his Winchester in his saddle scabbard. He had wrapped both weapons in his bedroll before leaving Chief Big Foot's camp in order not to provoke a confrontation of any kind with the cavalry over his possession of them. The soldiers, he understood, were far more comfortable guarding unarmed men. And, thus, far less likely to shoot.

The troopers drew rein and sat their saddles, watching as the people they had brought to Sitting Bull's camp under military guard began to unload travois and put up their lodges. When the last of the stragglers had arrived in the camp, the sergeant in charge of the escort ordered his men back to Camp Cheyenne.

Gabe dismounted and stood beside his sorrel, watching as the troopers forded the Grand River and rode south, the sight of their broad blue backs stirring anger in him.

But he refused to let himself vent that anger. They had a job to do and they did it, he told himself. Nobody got hurt. But his thoughts brought him no solace. Sky Walking Woman could have gotten hurt back in Big Foot's camp, he knew, when she bravely—or foolishly—retrieved Hears Thunder's rifle and gave it to her brother. If he hadn't broken the rifle in time . . . He didn't want to think about what might have—probably would have—happened since Colonel Sumner had been within seconds of ordering his men to open fire.

Thus ended the Ghost Dance, in bitter surrender. He had been yanked back from the Land of Many Lodges by the rude sound of soldiers storming the camp. The dancing had stopped. Fear had come to rest in the hearts of many of the dancers as women tried to protect their children, and men practiced a kind of brazen bravery in the face of the onslaught. But fear had dominated the day. Gabe had no doubt about that. Always the same old story, he mused. People fear people. Their fear breeds fury and fury breeds a climate in which bullets are bound to fly sooner or later, as they had almost flown in Big Foot's camp days ago.

"Maybe it is a good omen," Sitting Bull said, suddenly appearing at Gabe's side. "Today is Sunday—the white man's big medicine day—on which we come back to our campground and the soldiers disappear like summer's grass under winter's snows."

"Maybe so," Gabe said, unwilling to say more.

"I saw you fall to the ground during the dance. Did you have a good vision?"

"Yes, a good vision." A wonderful one. A marvelous one. Yellow Buckskin Girl's face appeared briefly in front of Gabe's bemused eyes as he remembered his vision.

"We will dance again," Sitting Bull stated firmly.

"Maybe it'd be a good idea if you decided to lay low for a spell," Gabe suggested.

"You mean the mice should be still until the cat sleeps."

"Something like that, yes."

"I will think about it."

"Good night," Gabe said and left Sitting Bull. After corralling his horse, he made his way to where Hears Thunder, Sky Walking Woman, and Warm Blanket were hard at work erecting their lodge in the darkness.

He pitched in to help them, saying, "I will spend the night in Strong Heart's lodge."

"You do not wish to be with us, Long Rider?" Hears Thunder asked, pausing in his labors. "You are welcome at our fire."

"I know I am and I thank you for that welcome. It's just that I've got some thinking to do and I think a whole lot better when I'm by myself."

Later, as Gabe sat cross-legged in front of the fire he had built for himself in Strong Heart's lodge, he stared into the flames and thought he could see Yellow Buckskin Girl's face in them. There she was, the woman he had lost and then found during the Ghost Dance but, paradoxically, the woman who remained lost to him.

He did not know what to think or what to believe about the Ghost Dance, or the promised messiah that the prophet, Wovoka, had said would come to the People to save them from the white men, to bring back the buffalo, and to make the world a place nearly as wonderful as was the Land of Many Lodges at the end of the Spirit Trail.

Was that any more preposterous a belief than the one many white men had in their messiah? The only difference that he could see between the two beliefs was that the red messiah had promised paradise on earth and the white messiah had promised paradise to those who believed in the life hereafter.

He was still turning the matter over in his mind when Sky Walking Woman slipped into the lodge.

He looked up at her and the bowl of food she carried in her hand.

"I brought this," she said in a small voice. "I thought Long Rider would be hungry."

"I am," he admitted. "To tell you the truth, I had forgotten to eat. I was too busy thinking, I guess."

She handed him the bowl and he began to eat, scooping up the blend of pemmican, roots, and seeds the bowl contained.

"I should not have given my brother the gun at Big Foot's camp," Sky Walking Woman said.

"I'd say you're right about that. Those soldiers, they tend to be in a hurry to shoot when they see something they don't like and they definitely don't like to see Indians with loaded guns in their hands."

"I am afraid." Sky Walking Woman's voice had trembled as she uttered the words.

Gabe didn't have to ask her of what she was afraid. He was sure he knew.

"The soldiers will come again. They always come again. Next time . . ."

As Sky Walking Woman's words trailed away, Gabe

recalled what Colonel Sumner had said to him at the end of their conversation in Big Foot's camp.

"Trouble lies ahead. But it is not your trouble. It is the Indians'."

"Come and sit down here by the fire," he said as he ate the last of the food Sky Walking Woman had brought him.

She did.

"Maybe things'll work out," he told her. "They usually do."

"But not always for the best."

"No, not always for the best." Gabe wished he could think of some reassuring words to offer her but none came to him. At least, none that he did not suspect of being misleading lies.

"I had a vision when we danced," Sky Walking Woman told him.

"You saw White Eagle, did you?"

Sky Walking Woman shook her head and gazed into the fire. "I saw you."

Gabe didn't know what to say.

"White Eagle is gone," she said. "One day you too will be gone."

He gave her a sidelong glance but could read nothing in her expression.

"When I came here tonight, it was not to bring you food. Not just that. I came here in the hope you and I could be together again. Before the time comes for you to leave us."

"Are you sure that's what you want?"

"It is what I want."

Gabe took her in his arms and held her close to him. As he did so, he knew the heat that was coursing through his body did not come from the fire alone. He felt himself stiffening as desire rose like a flood within him, urging him on, demanding that he do what he wanted so very much to do.

He slipped the blanket from Sky Walking Woman's shoulders and then lifted her to her feet. He stood before her, cupping her face in his hands as she looked up at him, surprised to find a tear forming in her right eye. With a thumb, he brushed it away.

"Now is not the time for sadness," he whispered in her ear. "Now is the time for joy."

"It is just that I know the sadness will come. When you are gone. I have known it before. When I lost my husband."

She surprised him then by dropping to her knees in front of him and hurriedly unbuttoning his jeans. His erection snapped up and out into the red light of the flames, throbbing, seeming to paw the air.

Sky Walking Woman took him into her mouth while her hand reached into his jeans to caress his testicles.

He stood there, looking down as her head bobbed back and forth, slowly at first, then faster and faster until he was forced to moan with pleasure. He clasped his hands together behind her head and thrust himself deep within her mouth that willingly took every inch he had to give.

It went on that way for a minute. Two minutes. Gabe groaned as hot waves of passion surged within him. The world seemed to have become centered in his groin. He looked down again. The wet, sucking sounds Sky Walking Woman was making were a counterpoint to the crackling of the fire. He withdrew from her mouth as he felt his climax coming and began to use his hand. She pushed it away and took him again into her mouth. Her lips tightened on him. He felt her tongue lave the underside of his erection . . .

He exploded.

His knees bent as a momentary weakness almost overcame him. He opened the eyes he had not realized he had closed, bent down, and helped Sky Walking Woman to her feet.

They embraced and then they lay down together on his fur coat. Gabe ran a finger down Sky Walking Woman's forehead, across the bridge of her nose, and down to its tip. He leaned over and nuzzled her neck, then helped her undress.

After he had undressed, the love play continued and grew in intensity, resulting in their passionate coupling. Afterward, with both of them spent, they slept, Gabe waking now and then and dozing off again, Sky Walking Woman sunk in deep slumber.

A shout awoke them some time later.

Gabe sat up and looked immediately at the tipi's smoke hole through which the first faint light of false dawn was spilling. Easy, he told himself. No need to be so skittish. The day's starting out and somebody's being noisy, that's all.

Another shout, louder this time. Then, still another one.

Gabe caught the name of Sitting Bull among the jumbled words of whoever it was who had been shouting.

"What is it?" Sky Walking Woman asked as she sat up beside Gabe and began to rub the sleep from her eyes. "Is something wrong?"

"That's what I'm going to find out," Gabe answered, hurriedly dressing and then pulling on his boots.

"Wait!" she called out to him as he was about to

leave the lodge. "Your ghost shirt." She held it out to him.

He hesitated and then, not wanting to offend her, took the shirt from her and put it on.

Once outside the tipi, he was amazed to see a crowd of people gathered around Sitting Bull's lodge. They were gesturing and talking excitedly among themselves. Beyond them were numerous armed Indian policemen, among whom Gabe recognized Sergeant Red Tomahawk and Lieutenant Henry Bull Head, whom he had met at Agent McLaughlin's office at the agency.

There sure is a whole big bunch of them, he thought. Dozens. A small army.

He ran to where the police had begun to herd the people away from Sitting Bull's lodge. Reaching the crowd, he elbowed his way through it and angrily freed Hears Thunder from the grip of two policemen by unceremoniously driving his fists into both men's faces.

"What's going on here?" he bellowed at the top of his voice.

"Stand Back!" Red Tomahawk ordered, brandishing his revolver.

"Stand *way* back!" Bull Head ordered him, the sidearm in his hand cocked and aimed at Gabe's gut. "You let us do what we came to do and nobody will get hurt. If you don't—keep what I'm about to tell you in mind. Colonel Drum at Fort Yates has sent two troops—that's two hundred men, in case you didn't know—under the command of Captain Fechet to back us up. What's more, Captain Fechet's bringing a Hotchkiss gun along with him and ought to be here just about any minute now. So go easy and everything will turn out fine."

Gabe forced himself to remain where he was, his

fists clenched at his sides. ''I want to know what this is all about,'' he muttered.

''We have our orders,'' Bull Head responded.

''What orders, dammit?'' Gabe shouted as the crowd behind him pressed forward.

''Agent McLaughlin has received orders from the military to arrest Sitting Bull,'' Bull Head replied. ''We have come to take him.''

Shouts of *''No!''* came from the people gathered around Gabe.

''What are you arresting him for?'' Gabe asked.

''Agent McLaughlin learned that Sitting Bull had left the reservation to attend the Ghost Dance at Chief Big Foot's camp. He notified the Department of the Interior. They contacted Colonel Miles. He gave the order for the arrest.''

''Where are you going to take him?'' Gabe asked.

''To the agency, where he will be imprisoned,'' Red Tomahawk answered.

''You will not take him!'' shouted a man on Gabe's left whom he had heard someone call Catch-the-Bear during the Ghost Dance.

At that moment, several policemen emerged from Sitting Bull's lodge with the medicine man.

''I will not go!'' Sitting Bull suddenly shouted and turned to reenter his lodge.

The policemen seized him and prevented him from doing so.

Gabe reached out, seized one of the policemen by the shoulder, spun him around, and sent his right fist flying into the man's startled face. As the lawman went down, Gabe jumped one of the other policemen but was promptly thrown off the officer's back. As he regained his balance, he saw, out of the corner of his eye,

Red Tomahawk raise his gun and bring the barrel slashing down. He felt it strike his temple and then he felt pain pound through his skull. His vision blurring, he staggered backward. As he did so, he saw Red Tomahawk step back behind Sitting Bull and Bull Head and another policeman take up positions flanking the medicine man. He was about to renew his attack upon the interlopers when Catch-the-Bear fired a shot from a revolver he had taken from beneath his blanket.

The round slammed into Bull Head's side, spinning the lieutenant around and almost knocking him to the ground. An instant later, Bull Head fired a round into Sitting Bull's body. Almost simultaneously Red Tomahawk shot Sitting Bull in the head.

Gabe stared in stunned disbelief as Sitting Bull dropped like a stone. He heard the sound of a shot fired from behind him and saw a policeman stagger and fall. He saw a policeman fire and down Catch-the-Bear.

Screams rent the dawn's air. Shouts resounded throughout the camp. Around Gabe, people surged forward past him to engage in hand-to-hand battle with the policemen. He plunged into the middle of the melee, wanting desperately to avenge Sitting Bull's death. There was no doubt in his mind that the great medicine man was dead. One look at the man's ghastly pallor and sightless staring eyes had been enough to convince him that life had forever fled from Sitting Bull's bleeding body.

He struck out at any uniformed body he could reach, hitting blindly, his lust for vengeance tearing him apart inside. He heard shots being fired but he didn't care. He continued battling along with the others, men and women both, some of them armed with guns, more of them armed with knives and war clubs which, like the guns, they had apparently kept hidden beneath their blankets during the confrontation.

Gabe slammed a fist into the gut of a policeman who had been holding a man by the hair while clubbing him with the butt of his revolver. The lawman grunted but did not let go of the man he had been battering. Gabe was about to strike another blow when a woman sprang forward and raised the already bloody knife she held in her hand. She brought it down and it bit into the policeman's back. His eyes widened in surprise. He moaned, dropping his sidearm. He tried and failed to reach behind him to seize the hilt of the woman's knife, which protruded from between his shoulder blades. He looked up at Gabe, an unanswerable question in his eyes and then, as blood began to ooze from between his lips, he fell forward and lay motionless on the ground.

The woman who had slain the policeman gave a wild war cry, ripped her knife from his body and ran, searching for another enemy to turn into a victim of the weapon she had just wielded so successfully.

Everywhere around him, Gabe saw the badly outnumbered policemen battling scores of attackers. He pushed his way through the combatants until he reached Sitting Bull's body, which he proceeded to drag out of the way so that it would not be trampled by those fighting one another. He had just placed Sitting Bull's corpse inside his tipi when he heard the sound of a bugle. He ducked out of Sitting Bull's lodge to find the cavalry cresting a low hill in the distance. At the same time as the cavalry began bearing down on the camp, the Hotchkiss gun the arriving troopers had brought fired two-pound shells and several people, both policemen and residents of the camp, were struck. Some died instantly. Others lay screaming and groveling on the ground, their blood staining it as they tried to rise, finally falling silent as Death claimed them too.

Outgunned. The word drummed in Gabe's mind. Spotting Hears Thunder in the distance, he cupped his hands around his mouth and yelled, *"Run!"* When Hears Thunder, who had just downed one of the Indian sergeants, cupped a hand around his ear to indicate that he had not heard, Gabe, instead of repeating what he had just shouted, pointed and then began to run toward the river, beckoning to Hears Thunder to follow him.

As he ran, he yelled to those he passed to follow him. Some heard him and obeyed. Others either ignored him or failed to hear him.

Followed now in his flight by a number of the other residents of the camp, Gabe glanced over his shoulder as he ran. When he saw the cavalry pursuing the fleeing men, women and children, he quickened his pace and loudly urged the others to do so.

"The timber!" he yelled, pointing to the trees growing on both sides of the river. "Take cover in the timber!"

It was all he could think of to do. The fleeing people had no horses. They couldn't hope to outdistance the mounted troopers who were so swiftly pursuing them. But in the meantime they would at least have a chance to hide, if not escape altogether.

He went crashing into the trees, Hears Thunder and the others not far behind him. He ran past the lodges that had been constructed there in the grove and on into the Grand River. With water splashing up around him, he bounded across the river to the thick stand of timber lining the far bank.

He stopped when he reached it and, panting breathlessly, shepherded the others into the trees, returning to the water to help several women, two of whom were carrying young children, ford the rushing river and climb to safety on the bank. When everyone, himself included, had taken cover in the trees, he turned to Hears Thunder, who had taken up a position by his side, and asked, "Have we any guns among us?"

Hears Thunder, instead of answering, crept swiftly away.

When he returned a few minutes later, he said, "We have five guns. Four revolvers. One rifle."

Gabe swore. Not much with which to go up against two troops of cavalry, he thought, as he continued watching the trees on the other side of the river, expecting at any moment to see the cavalry come riding out of them and into the river.

"Get the men with guns and form a skirmish line along here," he ordered Hears Thunder.

As Hears Thunder turned to leave, Gabe grabbed his arm. "Sky Walking Woman. Warm Blanket. Are they here?"

Hears Thunder shook his head and then he was gone.

Gabe crouched behind the trunk of a tree and kept his eyes on the timber on the opposite bank. He listened carefully but could hear no sound of horses. Was a surprise attack being planned by the army? He rose and tried to see through the trees to the left and right of his position but could not do so. He dispatched two men near him to check their flanks in case the troopers had circled around, intending to attack from those directions.

Hears Thunder returned and positioned the few armed men he had gathered in a skirmish line at the edge of the timber. Then he rejoined Gabe and both men, from their cover in the woods, gazed across the river.

Minutes passed and then still more minutes. Nearly an hour had gone by when a small band of women came out of the trees on the far side of the river and called out to those across the river from them. Some of the people with Gabe stepped out of the woods. Gabe, suspecting a trick, was about to call them back but he hesitated when he saw two women on the far bank wade into the river and then hurriedly ford it.

As they emerged wet and shivering from the cold water, he was among the people who hurried out to greet them.

"We bring word from the pony soldier chief," said one of the women. "He sent us here to tell you that you may all return to your homes in safety."

"They will not shoot us?" Hears Thunder asked, giving a contemptuous snort.

"They are going," the woman said. "They go back to Fort Yates. This thing I say is true."

The woman accompanying the one who had spoken nodded her head in confirmation of what her companion had said.

"What of the others who did not come over here with us?" Gabe asked the women, thinking of Sky Walking Woman and Warm Blanket.

"Those who had guns or clubs were disarmed by the pony soldiers," the woman replied. "They were not hurt."

"How many dead?" he asked.

"Sitting Bull is dead. So is his son, Crow Foot. Six others are also dead. All men."

"What about the soldiers?"

"Four killed. Two wounded."

Gabe turned to Hears Thunder. "We must go back and have funerals for Sitting Bull and the others."

The women, hearing what he had said, began to wail.

Gabe, believing that they were crying because of their grief, paid them little attention as he beckoned the others to follow him back across the river. But then, one of the women reached out and touched his arm.

"Yes, my sister?"

"We cannot place Sitting Bull in a funeral scaffold as is the custom," she told him.

"Why not?"

"The soldiers have taken his body away with them to Fort Yates."

Gabe silently swore. Then, "We will have a funeral for Sitting Bull. The old customs will be observed. Though we do not have his body, we will do what we can to honor him in death."

The women stared at him for a moment and then, asking no questions, they, along with Hears Thunder and all the others, walked into the cold water of the river and made their way to the other side and from there back to the camp.

There Gabe found Sky Walking Woman and her daughter huddled together with others who had not fled the camp when he and his band had done so. He wordlessly embraced both women as they softly wept. Then, gazing at the bodies of Crow Foot and the six others who had fallen in the brief but bloody battle, he gave instructions to some of the women to prepare the funeral feast. As the relatives of the dead began to prepare the bodies for their funerals, he stood watching.

Wailing, the mourners dressed the bodies in their finest attire, including spirit moccasins with beaded soles. In the dead men's hair were placed eagle feathers, badges of their past prowess in war. The faces of the dead were painted with dark blue stripes. In the case of one fallen warrior, the blue V of the White Buffalo Ceremony, to which he was apparently entitled, was painted on his face by a weeping young woman. Next, the dead men's most cherished possessions were gathered—their weapons, their war paint, their sacred amulets, their flutes. The bodies were wrapped in robes. Over the robes were placed folded tanned skins, all then tied securely with thongs to form large bundles.

Hears Thunder approached Gabe and said, ''I have been talking to the men. They do not want to stay here. They are afraid the soldiers will return and kill their women and children next time.''

''Where do they want to go?''

''To the Badlands in the southwest. What do you think of this idea, Long Rider? Should we go?''

Gabe considered the question. It was, he thought, entirely possible—perhaps even likely—that the Indian policemen, possibly accompanied by troopers the next time, would return to use even harsher methods to put down what they considered a potential uprising among what they must by now, as a result of the shooting in the camp, consider unruly Indians who presented a definite danger to them and to others in the area.

''We will go,'' he told Hears Thunder. Then, to the others gathered about who were engaged in the funeral preparations, he said, speaking loudly in order to be heard above the wailing of the mourning women, ''We do not have time to practice the customary four days of mourning. We will go to the Badlands where we will

be safe from the soldiers. Let us place the bodies where
they may rest and then let us leave this place of death.''

In response to his words, the people placed the
corpses on travois and took them to where they had
erected seven scaffolds. Behind them walked others,
each person leading a favorite horse that had belonged
to one of the deceased.

Gabe went to the corral and removed Sitting Bull's
favorite horse. Gripping a fistful of its mane, he led it
toward the scaffold that had been prepared for Sitting
Bull, but on which his body would not rest. On the way,
he spoke to one of the medicine man's wives, telling
her to bring her husband's lance, his drum, and his
medicine pouch.

When the procession had reached the scaffolds, Gabe
stood back as the bodies were placed in their resting
places and their burial bundles tied to the scaffold
beside them.

Sitting Bull's wife, to whom Gabe had spoken earlier, appeared at his side with her husband's burial bundle, some red paint, and a robe. She handed the paint
and robe to Gabe who proceeded to paint red marks on
Sitting Bull's horse and then to drape the dead man's
robe over the animal.

''The man we honor is not here,'' Gabe announced
when he had finished. ''But he is in our hearts. Look
close and it may be that you may see him there through
the eyes of a grieving relative or friend.''

The others fell silent. No woman wailed now. No
one so much as cleared his throat or coughed. Even the
children in the group stood silently, all their eyes on
Gabe.

Turning to Sitting Bull's horse, he drew his Colt and

spoke to the animal. "Grandchild, your owner thought a great deal of you and now he has died. He wants to take you with him, so go with him joyfully."

Gabe then shot the horse in the head at close range, aiming carefully so that the animal would die quickly and painlessly.

As the horse fell, both the men and women began to cry. Gabe waited a respectful few minutes and then he drew his knife, bent down, and cut off the horse's tail. Taking the burial bundle Sitting Bull's wife handed him, he placed both bundle and tail on the scaffold.

Then he sat down crosslegged on the ground and said, "Bring me wood."

When it had been brought to him in the form of several dry cedar branches, he took his knife and began to cut the branch into small pieces. These he sharpened. When he had finished, the men gathered around him and he proceeded to insert the sharp pegs he had fashioned in their arms and legs as a part of the funeral ritual—three pegs in each man's bared thigh, knee, and calf, and two pegs in each man's bared arm at the bicep and the forearm. When he had finished, he inserted the same number of pegs in his own arm and leg and then, as the other men were doing, he used his knife to cut short his hair in honor of the dead.

While the men were thus engaged, the women had taken their knives and made three slashes on their thighs and below their knees and then, as the men had just done, they, too, cut their hair.

Later, the scarification ceremony completed, Gabe ceremoniously pulled the pegs from each of the men's arms and legs, and from his own as well, before calling out to the people assembled around the scaffolds, "We must begin a long journey now to the Badlands in the south. We leave behind us the dead whom we loved and whom we will not forget. Gather all the food you can, those of you who want to come, and all your horses. Bring blankets and warm clothes. It is a long journey we must make. A cold one and a difficult one. Let us make ready for it.''

CHAPTER NINE

They had been on the move for nearly a week when, following the Indian Trail which they had picked up after crossing the border onto the Cheyenne River reservation, they came to Owl River.

There Gabe called a halt and they made camp for the night. He dispatched men to drag wood for fires from a nearby forest and sent women to haul water from the river. He watched as fires were built and food was prepared. Hears Thunder approached him and asked him to come to his fire and eat but he refused, saying he had things he had to do. In reality, he had refused Hears Thunder's invitation because he knew there was little food available and he did not want to make that little even less by taking any for himself. He had begun the habit of eating but once a day at the beginning of the southwest journey and now he did not eat at all on some days as the meager communal food supply dwindled daily.

He made the rounds of the sick, offering words of

encouragement to the aged and the very young, who were suffering from both malnutrition and severe fatigue, one ailment feeding upon the other to make each potentially deadly. He knew that some of those he visited would probably not reach the Badlands still so many days distant. That knowledge saddened him but his sadness was somewhat softened when he thought that the dead would have defeated their white enemies because in death, finally and paradoxically, they would have enjoyed their final triumph over their persecutors.

That night he posted pickets to make sure no Crow Indians who might be scouting for the army discovered them. If such scouts were seen, he told his sentries, they should be killed and word spread quickly throughout the camp that it was time to move and move quickly.

But the night passed with no alarm raised, for which he was grateful. As the morning star blazed in the pale blue sky, the camp awoke. An hour later, they were on the move again, some on horseback, many on foot, the latter slowing the southward trek.

It was not until the middle of the next day that they reached Cherry Creek, where the Indian Trail cut sharply to the west. They camped that night on Cherry Creek and in the morning buried three who had died during the night, taking no time for the proper rituals for fear of pursuit. Gabe helped the others dig shallow graves and pile stones upon them to protect the deceased from wolves and other animals.

Afterward, talking to Sky Walking Woman, whose cousin was one of the dead, he tried his best to console her but failed to do so. It pained him to see the worn expression on her face that was now gaunt from hunger. When she left him, he got his rifle and rode out in search of game. He rode for hours, until the sun was

almost down, but found no sign of any animals, not
even a rabbit. He did find a stand of young yellow pines
in the middle of which he dismounted and, using his
knife, hacked thick slabs of bark from the trees' trunks.
He cut off all of the tender inner bark, popped some of
it into his mouth and began to chew it, while packing
his saddlebags and coat pockets with the remainder.

Heading back to camp, he glanced at the sky and
saw the fat white clouds, which all had a bluish tinge
to them. Snow blossoms, he thought, using the name
he had heard white farmers use to describe such winter
storm clouds. Upon returning to camp, he distributed
the edible pine bark he had harvested, noticing as he
did so that the smoke from the fires, which had been
built mainly for warmth since there was little food left
to cook, hung low in the air instead of rising normally
and the horses seemed restless, unable to stand still for
long.

Two sure signs that snow's coming, he thought. And
cursed.

Next day, after an hour on the trail, the snow arrived.
Snowflakes drifted down, fat and seemingly frisky as a
light wind from the northeast played with them, sending them darting here, then swirling there.

The children greeted the snow with whoops of
delight. Soon, snowballs as well as snowflakes were
flying through the cold air which was causing the
horses' breath to emerge from their nostrils in great
moist clouds of steam.

Later, as the snow gradually thickened, the cold, it
seemed to Gabe, intensified. Still later, as the temperature continued to drop and the snow continued to fall,
he reached behind him and, rummaging around in his
saddle bag, came up with a sheepskin-lined cinch strap

which he fastened around the lower part of his face to help keep out the cold and his buckskin gloves, which he put on. He pulled his hat down low on his forehead to ward off some of the snow that was flying into his face as the wind grew even stronger.

Around him, others were unpacking blankets from the belongings they had lashed to travois and wrapping themselves in them in an effort to keep warm. Some covered their heads with the blankets, leaving only a narrow space through which they peered at the snow that was turning the world around them white.

A white nightmare, Gabe thought an hour later as the storm matured into a full-fledged blizzard. He drew rein and dismounted. Hunkering down, he took a metal waterproof container of matches from his pockets and lit several, letting each one burn down until it almost scorched his fingers. He used the charred matches to blacken the skin beneath his eyes in order to keep from going snow-blind. Then he removed a slicker from his saddle bag and gave it to a woman who was trudging through the snow near him, a woman who had only a single nearly threadbare blanket to cover herself with.

A man rode up to him. "We stop, yes? Find shelter?"

"We're in open country now," Gabe pointed out, shouting at the top of his voice to be heard above the whine of the wind. "There's no shelter that I can see anywhere near us and if we stop, this killing cold's going to get to a lot of people."

As if to prove his point, a young girl suddenly slumped down in the snow that was piling up on the ground and slowly lowered her head until her face was buried in it.

Gabe spurred his horse and rode over to her. He

reached down, lifted her to her feet, and then shook her violently. When her eyes remained closed, he shook her again even more violently and was gratified to see her eyes open. He was even more gratified to see the smile that crept slowly over her face.

"Long Rider," she murmured.

"Keep moving," he told her. "Don't give up. I know it's cold. But—"

"Want to sleep," she said.

"Don't!"

She walked on. Gabe beckoned to a woman nearby and pointed to the girl. The woman went and put an arm around her and the pair moved on through the snow that was being blown hard now and beginning to drift. He returned to the man who had spoken to him earlier. "It's better for us if we keep going," he told him. "Keep your eyes peeled for anybody who's on the verge of freezing like that girl I spotted just now. Don't let them stop. Keep them moving. If they stop, chances are they'll freeze to death."

Gabe, as the man left him, reached down and brushed the snow from his sorrel's eyes when the horse stumbled. He found them coated with ice. Taking off a glove and holding one hand first over one eye and then the other, he managed to melt the ice and the horse moved on almost smartly, as if it were immensely relieved to have been freed of the crystals that had partially blinded it.

It began to grow warmer and Gabe began to hope that the snow would end. It didn't. It turned to sleet. Then, to make matters even worse, the wind's velocity increased and the temperature began to fall again.

The result was a crust of ice that formed on the top of the fallen snow, a sharp crust which cut the horses' legs as they plowed through it, sending blood streaming down to redden the snow and mark the trail as they rode over it and then to vanish as still more snow fell.

The riders in the grim procession bent over their horses' necks to try to shield themselves from the wind. Those on foot, huddled shapes that looked hardly human, walked grimly on, putting one exhausted foot in front of the other. No one spoke. The children clung to their parents, their snowball fights long since forgotten, one or two of them whimpering under the icy lash of the wind that stirred up the snow which continued falling relentlessly.

Gabe let his sorrel pick its own pace, the reins hanging limply in his hand. He heard the animal's heavy breathing and he saw the way the nearly exhausted animal occasionally dropped its head until its nose was nearly touching the snow. He quickly dismounted and once again brushed the snow and ice away from the horse's eyes. Then, leading the animal at a slow pace, he began to walk through the wind-whipped snow. Billows of steam shot from the sorrel's nostrils. Its sides heaved. Snow melted on its hot sweating body and ran down its legs. Icicles began to form on the horse's body as its sweat froze. The icicles gradually thickened and then fell of their own weight, tearing loose patches of hide as they did so.

Around Gabe, horses, some of them gone lame as a result of their desperate journey through the ice-encrusted snow, foundered. One fell. Two others refused to move, their eyes frozen shut.

He glanced around at the people, nearly all of whom had halted to stand dumbly as if finally defeated by the overpowering elements.

We're done for if we don't get moving, he thought.

But these people don't look like they're willing or even able to put one foot in front of another. He tried to think of something to do. There was no shelter from the storm anywhere near them. There was no way of escaping it or its cruel companion, the fleshfreezing cold that numbed limbs and one's will to fight it. His gaze drifted to the fallen horse and it was then that the plan came to him. Would it work? He had no way of knowing. But he was willing to try it in the hope that it would work.

He strode over to the downed horse whose sides were heaving but whose eyes were glazed. As he came closer to it, he was able to see its right front leg, which protruded at an ugly angle from a snowdrift. Blue white bone showed through the broken leg's torn flesh.

He drew his revolver, cocked it, and fired, sending a bullet boring into the broken-legged horse's brain, killing the animal instantly.

Blowing smoke away from the barrel of his gun, he holstered the weapon, turned to face the people watching him, pulled down the cinch covering his mouth and spoke a single word which the wind almost whipped away before it could be heard: "Food."

But the people heard what he said. They looked from him to the horse. Then a cry went up, a weak one, but one that was an affirmation of life in the face of death.

As the snow continued to fall, but less heavily now, the people pounced like wild animals upon the body of the dead horse while Gabe watched. Knives appeared and the people wielding them began to peel the hide from the dead horse. Steam arose from its hot body to twist upward into the falling snow where it swiftly disappeared. Blood spattered the snow surrounding the carcass. Bones were bared and then severed. Haunches were removed.

A fire was built and sticks were sharpened to serve as spits.

The odor of warm blood invaded Gabe's nostrils as he continued watching the people tear pieces of dripping flesh from the animal's body. Saliva suddenly flooded his mouth and he realized how hungry he was, how *ravenous* he was. He suppressed the urge to reach down and rip free a piece of horseflesh and devour it raw.

The people speared gobs of meat with their sticks and held them over the flame, laughing now and talking among themselves, seemingly unmindful of the still-falling snow that enveloped them, the snow that melted as it landed on the gutted body of the horse.

Gabe became aware of the fact that a woman was calling his name. He looked at the left and saw Sky Walking Woman beckoning to him. He went to her and she sliced a piece of meat from the horse's left shoulder, speared it on the end of a stick, and handed it to him with a weak smile.

He took it from her, thanked her, and hunkered down next to the fire to hold the meat over the flames as the others were all doing, their eyes glittering like the eyes of demons in the fire's reflected light. He turned the stick in his hands to sear the meat on the outside so the blood would not drip from it and dry it out. Moments later, the meat slipped from his stick and fell into the fire. He jabbed at it several times before succeeding in retrieving his meal.

All around the fire, people were gobbling down cinder-coated pieces of roasted horseflesh, eating with a kind of wildness in their eyes as their teeth tore at the meat and blood stained their lips and cheeks and chins.

Gabe, when his meat was roasted, bit into it, tearing pieces of it free. Not taking time to chew them thoroughly, he swallowed them greedily, compelled to do so by the force of his hunger. Others around him were doing the same thing, all of them greedily gorging themselves on the meat and, he thought, taking in renewed hope and the will to live along with their meal.

Some time later, when only bones adorned with bits of gristle jutted up from the snow, one of the women shouted and pointed skyward.

Gabe looked up, blinking away the snowflakes that fell into his eyes, and then rising, he shouted with joy as the woman had just done.

A round brassy disk was faintly visible through the veil of snow.

The people, their hunger satisfied, stood and watched in almost total silence as the sun grew stronger and the storm grew weaker. They cheered loudly and clapped their hands as the snow suddenly stopped and the sun burst into bright yellow life.

Later, after consulting together, they decided to remain where they were for the remainder of the day and make camp for the night that was swiftly coming.

Gabe went to his horse and examined the wounds on the sorrel's legs and hide, regretting the fact that he had neither whiskey nor honey to apply to them, both of which were good antiseptics. Making do with what he had, he used snow to cleanse the animal's wounds. In the process, he deliberately caused them to bleed in the Indian way so that the bleeding itself would help to cleanse the lesions, some of which were severe, especially on the horse's front legs.

He had just completed the task when Sky Walking Woman came running toward him, the blanket she wore wrapped around her body, flapping out behind her.

"What's wrong?" he asked her as she came to a breathless halt in front of him.

Out of breath, she could at first only point in the direction from which she had come.

Gabe followed her as she retraced her steps and found Hears Thunder holding his niece in his arms, a worried expression on his face.

"Warm Blanket cannot see!" Sky Walking Woman told Gabe. "She has gone blind!"

Gabe gestured and Hears Thunder stepped aside. "Warm Blanket," he said, "Look at me."

When she did, Gabe waved a hand in front of her face. No reaction. She simply stared straight ahead.

"She's all right," he said.

"She is not!" Hears Thunder exclaimed. "She can see nothing!"

"She's just snow-blind," Gabe said. "She'll be all right in a little while. Just keep her out of the way so she doesn't get injured by a horse or something like that. Her sight will come back soon. What you can do for her is, make salt poultices to put on her eyes. That'll speed up the return of her sight.

"Warm Blanket, you just sit tight," he continued, patting her on the shoulder. "Don't be scared. Everything's going to be fine."

"Are you sure, Long Rider?" she asked hesitantly, her brow furrowing.

"I'm sure. I wouldn't lie to you, not about something like this."

"I believe you, Long Rider."

• • •

In the morning, Gabe went to see Warm Blanket as soon as he awoke. As he had predicted, she was fine. He learned that Hears Thunder had scouted about and found a salt lick and Sky Walking Woman had used the salt he had brought her to make poultices for her daughter's eyes as Gabe had advised.

"I can see clearly now," Warm Blanket told him.

"And isn't it a bright and beautiful world that there is to see this morning?" he asked with a smile and a gesture. "Look up there at that sky. Blue as a jay and not a cloud in it."

"The snow is beginning to melt," Sky Walking Woman observed, pointing to the branches of the trees which had been ice-encrusted but now had begun to shed their silvery sheaths in the form of steadily dripping water as the sun climbed higher in the sky.

They moved out then, most of the group on foot now. By the time the sun had reached its meridian, they had arrived at the Cheyenne River. Gabe gave orders that those travelers with horses were to help the others who were on foot across the river that was partially frozen but not solid enough to walk across.

Mounted men, following Gabe's order, took one passenger at a time across the river and then returned for another one. No one mentioned stopping. No one spoke of building cooking fires because there was no food left to cook. There was only the trail ahead and the threat of pursuit by soldiers behind them. There was no turning back. They could only go forward toward whatever awaited them in the south. They numbered thirty-nine men, women, and children who traveled on with fear marching with them, fear which caused them to often look over their shoulders toward what might be on their backtrail.

But when others came on the following day, it was not from the north but from the west. And the others who came were not soldiers but a band of Chief Big Foot's Miniconjou Sioux numbering three hundred strong.

"How," he said to Big Foot, who responded with, "You come so soon again to the south, Long Rider. What brings you here this time?"

Gabe dismounted and explained to Big Foot about the killing of Sitting Bull and the fears of the Hunkpapa which had led to the flight of many from the Standing Rock reservation.

"My friend is dead?" Big Foot asked, apparently unable or unwilling to believe the truth.

"He is dead," Gabe confirmed.

Big Foot turned and spoke to a man at his side.

The man moved out into the throng of people to spread the bad news that Gabe had brought.

"Where do you go now?" Big Foot asked.

"To the Badlands in the southwest. There are many places to hide there from the soldiers."

"You think the soldiers will come after you?"

"I think there's a good chance they will, yes. Big Foot, I hate to ask you this but we could use some food if you've got any to spare."

"I have some. You are welcome to it. We go now to agency headquarters near Fort Bennett on the Missouri River to get our monthly rations. Come with us and we will give you some of our food."

"I thank you for being willing to share your rations with us, Big Foot. But I think I'm going to have to turn down your generous offer."

"Why is that, Long Rider?"

"I don't think it would be wise for us to go anywhere

near Fort Bennett or Cheyenne River agency. They may well have gotten word by now that we've jumped the reservation and I don't think we'd be welcome. In fact, I think we'd find ourselves in the guardhouse at Fort Bennett before we knew what had hit us.''

Big Foot nodded thoughtfully. ''We will give you some of our food for your journey.''

Big Foot gave an order and one of his men moved through the band of Miniconjou, collecting from them what food they could spare for Gabe and his small band.

But, before the food could be turned over, the clear, cold air carried the sound of pounding hooves to Gabe and the others.

He looked to the west from which direction the ominous sound had come and saw Eighth Cavalry troopers approaching.

''Sumner,'' Big Foot muttered. ''Maybe the Colonel comes to see if Big Foot holds another Ghost Dance.''

The chief's words were bitter despite their inherent humor and Gabe noted that there was no smile on the old man's face.

Sky Walking Woman appeared out of the crowd with Hears Thunder right behind her. Both of them came to stand next to Gabe. With him and the others, they silently watched the blue wave of troopers ride up to them and halt.

Colonel Sumner, his hands resting on his saddle horn, surveyed the throng and then glanced inquiringly at Gabe. When Gabe said nothing, he turned to Big Foot. ''Where do you happen to be headed, Chief?''

''To Fort Bennett to get our monthly rations.''

''I see you've got company for your journey.'' Sumner waved a hand, the gesture encompassing the Hunkpapa who had gathered around Gabe as Sky Walking

Woman and Hears Thunder had just done. "Bad company," Sumner added in a surly tone of voice.

"We met a little while ago," Big Foot declared. "They—"

"They are some of Sitting Bull's hostiles," Sumner snapped.

"Call them what you will," Big Foot said calmly. "I call them poor people. They have no food and only a few clothes. They are footsore and weary. I have tried to help them."

"Oh, is that so?" Sumner asked, arching his eyebrows as he stared down at Big Foot. "It's not that all you troublemakers have decided to join forces for some as yet unknown but no doubt nefarious purpose."

Big Foot said nothing.

"Look, Colonel," Gabe said, "We haven't caused you or anybody else any trouble and we've no intention of doing so. We'll get on our way and out of your hair right now."

As Gabe put his foot in a stirrup and was about to swing into the saddle, Sumner said, "Hold it, Conrad."

Gabe looked up at him.

"I note that despite your declaration just now of having nothing but peaceable intentions, you're well-armed. You've got a Winchester in your saddle scabbard and a Colt hanging on your hip. How do those weapons fit with your so-called peaceable intentions?"

"Colonel, you know a man needs a gun or two out here on the plains. He's got to feed himself, and shooting himself some meat on the hoof is one of the ways he goes about doing that. Then, too, there are some far from friendly folks he might run into out here and a gun comes in handy at a testy time like that."

"Sergeant," Sumner said, and gestured at Gabe. "Relieve this man of his weapons."

"Now it's your turn to hold it, Colonel," Gabe said angrily but fell silent when the sergeant riding next to Sumner dismounted, drew his Army Colt and leveled it at him.

"Proceed, Sergeant," Sumner directed.

"Your gunbelt, sir," the sergeant said to Gabe after he had removed Gabe's rifle from its saddle scabbard.

Gabe, his cold gray eyes on Sumner, unbuckled his cartridge belt and handed it to the sergeant who then withdrew.

"I have orders to arrest Big Foot," Sumner then announced. "The military authorities do not trust you, Chief—you and your ridiculous ghost dancing. I have orders to take you to Camp Cheyenne."

Turning his gaze on Gabe again, Sumner continued, "You, Conrad, and those hostiles you're traveling with—I'm taking the whole kit and caboodle along with me to Camp Cheyenne."

Gabe decided it would do no good to protest. He was now weaponless, and the troopers under Sumner's command were heavily armed. He made up his mind to bide his time. Perhaps there would be a chance to escape from the army at some later time. Or perhaps the whole matter could be resolved peacefully in some other fashion once they got to Camp Cheyenne. The one thing he didn't want to do was make any trouble here and now which might well result in a repetition of the deadly confrontation that had occurred earlier in Sitting Bull's camp which had led to the medicine man's death along with others as innocent as he was.

"Move your people out, Chief," Sumner peremptorily ordered Big Foot.

Gabe, fearing a protest from the elderly leader, leaned toward him and said in a low tone, "It might be best if we went along with these soldier boys for now."

"What about our rations?" Big Foot asked the colonel.

"There will be sufficient food for you and your people at Camp Cheyenne."

"Then we will go with you."

Gabe wasn't sure whether Big Foot had decided to obey the colonel because of the promise of food or because of his own recommendation to avoid trouble that might lead to disaster. It didn't matter one way or another. What did matter was the fact that there was not about to be any shooting. He swung into the saddle and rode out with the others, heading west and flanked by two long lines of troopers.

The march was made mostly in silence. Occasionally a child cried, but otherwise the journey across the plains was made in an almost soundless fashion in the way of a people who have nothing more to say because all that is left to say is too painful to put into words.

Defeated, Gabe thought as he moved west with the others. That's what the People are and if there is indeed a messiah coming to save them he'd better get a move on because before long there's not going to be anybody left to save. They're a dying race, he thought bitterly as he rode slowly on past hummocks and trees and piles of frost-cracked boulders, the sky blue above, the snow below continuing to melt, thus making the journey less arduous than had been the trek through the blizzard. The white man's robbed the People of the buffalo, he thought, of the land they once freely roamed, and, worst of all, of their dignity and self-respect.

They traveled throughout the rest of the day, stopping twice before sunset to let the very old and the very young rest. That night they camped on a tributary of the Cheyenne River that jutted southward from the main body of water. Their evening meal consisted of army rations—hardtack, boiled beans, and watery coffee.

Gabe ate his portion of the food the soldiers had distributed in the company of Hears Thunder, Sky Walking Woman, and Warm Blanket. It was Warm Blanket who asked him, "What will they do with us when we reach Camp Cheyenne?"

What could he tell her? The truth was all he could manage: "I don't know."

"Perhaps when its gets dark," Hears Thunder said softly, "we could slip away."

"We are not far from the Badlands," Sky Walking Woman pointed out. "If we went in the night when they cannot see us and if we went quickly—"

"They'll have pickets posted," Gabe said. "Those fires they've built around the camp's perimeter—they'll see to it that they're burning real bright come darkness. No, I think the best thing we can do is play along with Colonel Sumner for now. Wait and see what him and his bosses have got up their sleeves."

"Some of Big Foot's people have guns," Hears Thunder whispered to Gabe. "They showed them to me on the trail. There are more of us than there are soldiers. We could wait until most of them are asleep tonight. Then we could kill the pickets one by one and overpower the others because we are so many."

Gabe said, "I don't mean to say what you're talking about won't work. It very well might. But there are a couple of things to consider before you go on down that road, Hears Thunder. One of them is this. Exactly how many guns have the Miniconjou got? The second thing to keep in mind is all the Hunkpapa men including you, are worn to a frazzle. Now, about the guns. Do you know how many there are?''

"I do not know but I believe there are not many," he admitted with evident reluctance.

"That's my point," Gabe responded with the same reluctance. "Bear in mind, too, that Chief Big Foot's an old man and I for one don't think he's up to leading an attack."

"I could lead it," Hears Thunder declared.

"I bet you'd do a good job of it too. But I say it's too risky. Maybe even foolhardy considering the way things are on our side at the moment."

"I am afraid to be here," Warm Blanket murmured. "There are so many soldiers. It is almost like it was in our camp before. Then there were policemen. Now there are soldiers. Otherwise, it is much the same and it makes me afraid."

Sky Walking Woman put an arm around her daughter. "It will be all right," she promised. "Long Rider is with us."

Inwardly Gabe cringed at her words, knowing there was little or nothing he could do to make things right for all of them. He was but one man. One man without a gun.

The journey continued the following day. Colonel Sumner called a halt at midday and they made their nooning in a grove of cedars that offered some protection from the wind.

Gabe, hunkered down by himself sipped coffee from a tin cup as he watched Big Foot rise in the distance and walk stiffly toward where Colonel Sumner sat on a slanted boulder, his booted legs crossed as he gnawed on a piece of hardtack.

When the chief reached the colonel, Gabe saw him speak to the man in an animated fashion and point first to the north and then to his band of Miniconjou Sioux.

The conversation went on for several minutes. When it ended, Big Foot made his way back to his band, a broad smile on his face.

Gabe, wondering what had been discussed to make the chief smile, rose and went over to him. "What was that all about between you and the colonel?" he asked.

"I told him I had decided not to go to Camp Cheyenne. I told him I had decided to go home. I told him our village is just north of here. I told him we would go there and live peacefully and I told him that I had decided he had no right to remove us from our land as he has been trying to do."

Gabe, taken aback by Big Foot's speech, asked, "What did the colonel have to say to all that?"

"He said we may go home."

"What about Sitting Bull's people?"

"I told him you would all come home with us. I did not tell him that once the soldiers were gone, you would continue to journey south again until you reached the Badlands where there are no soldiers."

Big Foot smiled.

So did Gabe.

CHAPTER TEN

Excitement greeted them when they arrived at Big Foot's camp in the north late that afternoon. Those who had remained in camp instead of accompanying the chief and the others on their trip to the agency to collect the monthly rations were in an uproar. People ran about from one tipi to another, talking excitedly among themselves and casting apprehensive glances to the east.

Big Foot, coughing as he had begun to do during the trip back to his camp, rode up to the nearest of his people and asked them what was wrong.

One of his men replied, "Deer Standing Still has returned from the agency today. He says there is talk there of sending soldiers to our village. Maybe they come today. Maybe tomorrow. But they are coming. That is what Deer Standing Still says."

Big Foot turned to Gabe who had been riding by his side. "Will they give us no peace? Will they chase us into the great water that lies in the land where the sun sets?"

Gabe gave no answer to Big Foot's questions.

"Is this tale true?" Big Foot asked the man who had just spoken to him. "I do not know," the man replied. "But Deer Standing Still says it is true. He says he heard a soldier say it is so at the agency."

"Why are the soldiers coming?" Big Foot asked and coughed.

"No one knows."

"Bring Deer Standing Still to me," Big Foot ordered as he got down from his horse.

When the man had been brought, the chief questioned him carefully and Deer Standing Still told essentially the same story that the other man had just recounted.

Deer Standing Still had been at the agency to await the distribution of rations. He had seen soldiers come there from Fort Bennett. He had heard one of them say that he and many other soldiers were being sent to Chief Big Foot's village. No, Deer Standing Still did not know why the soldiers were coming. No, he did not know how many soldiers were coming nor did he know when they would arrive. He did know that he and everyone else was afraid of what would happen to them when the soldiers came.

Big Foot turned to Gabe. "We cannot stay here any longer. We will go with you to the Badlands."

"Chief, are you sure you're strong enough to travel all that way? I've heard you coughing—"

"I have pain here." Big Foot touched his chest. "My head is on fire." He touched his forehead. "But, yes, I am strong enough to travel. I *must* be strong enough. If I do not go the soldiers will come and maybe then I will die. Maybe all of us will die if we do not go away."

• • •

They left the following morning at first light, Big Foot bundled up in a heavy coat and wearing a scarf over his head which was tied beneath his chin.

Gabe rode in front of the long procession of people who were burdened with their possessions wrapped in skins and cloth bundles, most of them pulling their tipis and other wordly goods on travois through what snow still remained on the ground.

On his right rode Big Foot. He noted the way the old man's hand had begun to tremble but said nothing about it. He didn't like the look of the chief's eyes, the way they seemed to have sunk into his skull. The sheen of sweat that coated the man's face made him uneasy.

Big Foot rode on, his back almost straight, his dull gaze focused directly ahead of him. At times, Gabe thought he saw a faint light glowing in those old eyes. What does he see, he wondered. A vision of a peaceful refuge down south in the Badlands? Or a vision maybe of some place where the bluecoats will at last leave him alone?

The day passed slowly from sunrise to sunset and on to a night of hunger and privation, a night of bad dreams and worse realities.

One of the latter was Death, which claimed a woman and a child belonging to Gabe's band of by now badly bedraggled people. He helped dig the shallow graves in which the two emaciated corpses were placed and then the group moved doggedly on.

Chief Big Foot became sicker and Gabe arranged for him to travel lying on one of the band's travois. He covered the chief with several blankets but still the old man shivered. Shivered and coughed and sweated. Pneumonia, Gabe thought but he did not speak the

word. On the day they made camp on Bull Creek, Big
Foot asked for Yellow Bird, the shaman, and Gabe went
and got him.

Yellow Bird knelt beside the ailing chief, unwrapped
his medicine bundle, and proceeded to try to drive away
the demon that had possessed his chief. Waving painted
feathers and rattling human finger bones in a bowl, he
fought the demon, tried to sing him out of the frail body
lying on the travois before him, struggled valiantly with
the evil spirit by means of magical words and deeds.

To Yellow Bird's shame, the old man only grew
worse.

But the Badlands were not far away now. Gabe,
kneeling on the ground beside Big Foot after Yellow
Bird had gone, told the old man so and he thought he
saw the chief's eyes brighten slightly at the news.

"We'll be there in another couple of days or so," he
assured Big Foot. "Then we can stop and take some
time to catch our breath. Once we've gotten our bear-
ings, we can move deeper into the Badlands. There's
a lot of places in there where nobody'll ever be able to
find us. Only an eagle flying high up in the sky will
know we're there and he'll only know it if he looks at
least twice."

Big Foot smiled. Then, he slept.

Gabe was still kneeling beside the travois supporting
the sick man when Sky Walking Woman joined him.

"Death makes the journey with us, Long Rider,"
she said in a flat voice that was devoid of all emotion.

"So does Life," Gabe countered. "Sure, it's been a
hard trek and it's going to be hard for awhile longer."
He got up and placed his hands on Sky Walking Woman's shoulders. "Don't you think about giving up, you
hear me?"

"I am so tired. But when I try to sleep I see him in my dreams. Death. He rides a black horse which has eyes of ice."

Gabe, frowning, placed the back of his hand against Sky Walking Woman's forehead. No fever. So she had not been hallucinating, only dreaming as she claimed.

"How's Warm Blanket holding up?"

"She is courageous. She tells me I must not give up, that we will soon be safe in the Badlands."

"She's right," Gabe assured Sky Walking Woman and had only just done so when Warm Blanket's prediction was proven wrong by the sudden arrival in the camp of a troop of cavalry.

Sky Walking Woman began to shudder. Then to cry. She stood beside Gabe watching the soldiers surround the camp and, as the tears flowed from her eyes, she made no sound as she wept.

The man in command of the troopers, a major, rode around the perimeter of the camp, deploying his troops. When he had returned to his starting point, he seemed to notice Gabe for the first time. He sat his saddle, staring at Gabe for a long moment, and then, putting spurs to his mount, he rode over to where Gabe stood beside Sky Walking Woman.

"I am Major Whitside, sir," he declared, drawing rein. "May I ask your name?"

"Conrad."

"May I also ask what you, a white man, are doing in the camp of these hostiles?"

Gabe couldn't help it. He sighed, a sense of weariness almost overcoming him that was not physical but spiritual. "Major Whitside, you call these folks 'hostiles'. How come you can't see that they're just people the same as you and me and then call them that. Calling them hostiles is no way to get along with them. It makes you scared of them and they're already scared of you."

"I did not come here to be lectured by you, Mr. Conrad. I merely asked what you were doing in a hos— in an Indian encampment."

"These people are friends of mine." Gabe knew his answer was only part of the truth. But maybe it would satisfy Major Whitside.

The major thoughtfully stroked his chin, his eyes still fixed on Gabe. "I find your presence here a most unusual matter, I must say. But never mind about that. Mr. Conrad, you are free to go."

"Free to go? Major, I'm not going anywhere."

"I have received orders from General Miles, as have the commanders of all cavalry units here in Sioux country, to seek out and apprehend Chief Big Foot's band of renegades who, I'm told, also include a number of Sitting Bull's people."

Gabe wondered if Whitside's use of the word 'people' had been a deliberate choice instead of 'hostiles' or if the major had merely used it thoughtlessly.

"Well, Major, it looks to me like you've done what you set out to do."

Whitside scanned the camp. "It appears to me that these people would have done well to remain on their reservations. They look half-starved, some of them half-dead in fact."

"It's been no party for them on the reservations, Major. How the hell can it be? They don't get enough food from the government. They don't have any decent medical care. Chief Big Foot over there is sick with what I'd say is probably pneumonia. He got about as good care on the trail from his medicine man as he would be likely to get back on the Cheyenne River reservation. Then there's—''

''I repeat, Mr. Conrad, I am not here to be lectured by you.''

''What are you here for, Major, now that you've caught us?''

''I am here to escort these Indians south, where they can be safely contained. But you, Mr. Conrad, as I said before, are perfectly free to go.''

''I'm staying, Major.''

''Suit yourself. Perhaps you will be good enough to tell these people for me, since I don't speak their language, that they are to break camp and move out.''

Gabe, his arm around Sky Walking Woman, walked away and began to spread the word that Whitside had just given him.

He had not gone far when Sky Walking Woman halted, pointed, and cried, ''Long Rider, look!''

Gabe looked and saw Big Foot struggling to rise from the travois on which he had been lying. In his right hand was a long stick topped by a torn piece of white muslin. As Gabe hurried toward the chief with Sky Walking Woman, Big Foot managed to get to his feet. When Gabe reached him and tried to help him, Big Foot waved him away.

Then the chief, half-tottering, walked to where Major Whitside was conversing with two of his officers.

Gabe and Sky Walking Woman followed him.

When Big Foot reached the soldiers, he said, ''I am Big Foot. I have come on behalf of my people and those from Sitting Bull's band of Hunkpapa Sioux. I ask you to treat us with respect and we will obey your orders. We are a proud people and do not want to be treated like dogs.''

"You will be given every courtesy, Chief," Whitside said, surprising Gabe. "But you are ill. Perhaps you should—"

Whitside never got to finish whatever it had been that he was about to say. He was interrupted by Big Foot whose eyes, Gabe noticed, had begun to blaze with the fire of fever.

"See there in the sky," Big Foot intoned, pointing. "There does he come from the land where the sun sets—the messiah. He comes to his children and with him comes the buffalo. See them there, that big herd that has no end. See the hand the messiah stretches out to me. I reach out. I take it—"

Gabe seized Big Foot as he lapsed into unconsciousness, preventing him from falling to the ground.

"The poor devil," Whitside muttered under his breath. "Lieutenant Kendrick, help Mr. Conrad with Chief Big Foot. Do what you can for the man."

Lieutenant Kendrick and Gabe carried Big Foot back to his travois and gently laid him down upon it as around them the People had begun to break camp and prepare for their trek southward.

Gabe stood in the morning sunlight on a slight rise and gazed at the new camp that was being set up a short distance west of Wounded Knee Creek. The work was almost finished; most of the tipis had been erected. The scene looked incredibly peaceful to him except for the potentially deadly presence of Major Whitside's troopers who had been joined on the trail south by four more cavalry troops under the command of Colonel James Forsythe, which brought the two officers' combined force to a total of four hundred and seventy men.

In the center of the camp, someone had hoisted Big

Foot's white flag of peace. Behind the camp a dry ravine which ran east into the creek. In front of the camp,
on a slight rise, a battery of four Hotchkiss guns had
been put in place, all of them trained directly on the
camp.

In front, behind, and on both flanks of the camp
were soldiers, a number of them dismounted and stationed directly in front of the camp at a distance of only
a few yards from the nearest tipi.

Major Whitside joined Gabe on the rise. "I don't
want you to think, Mr. Conrad, that I am an unfeeling
man. I wanted you to know that I have spoken to Colonel Forsythe who, by the way, is now in command of
this operation, about the poor physical condition of
Chief Big Foot. I asked him to supply a camp stove to
keep the Chief warm and he has complied with my
request."

Gabe nodded, his eyes on the army tent that had been
put up to house Big Foot and his wife. "That was
thoughtful of you, Major, though I don't know how
much good it's going to do the old man at this point."

Whitside nodded. "As you say, he is an old man."

Gabe gave the major a sidelong glance. "Now I suppose you're going to tell me he lived a long life and a
good one." As Whitside started to protest, Gabe silenced him by saying, "He did live a good life, like all
of these people did before we—before white men—came
to wreak havoc with their lives. But his life now, it's
not worth spit on a stick."

"The Sioux have slaughtered many of us, Mr. Conrad, civilians as well as soldiers," Whitside pointed out
somewhat testily. "Surely you are aware of that."

"Oh, I'm aware of it, all right. But, Major, I'm sure
you're aware of the fact that those of us the Sioux

slaughtered wouldn't have died if they'd stayed where
they were and just minded their own damned business!''

Whitside said nothing.

"Major, I've been noticing the troops you and the
colonel have got on armed guard around the camp. They
look to me, a whole lot of them do, like nothing more
than boys.''

"They are young and, as I suspect you are implying,
they are also largely unseasoned. Most of them have
never engaged in an armed encounter with Indians before.''

Gabe turned to face Whitside. "Is that what you call
what's going on here? An armed encounter?''

"In a manner of speaking, yes.'' Whitside cleared
his throat. "I came here, Mr. Conrad, for another reason, not just to tell you about the camp stove that has
been supplied to Chief Big Foot.''

Gabe waited.

"Colonel Forsythe is planning to disarm the Indians
this morning. I suggested to him that I might be able
to enlist your cooperation in the operation. I thought
perhaps you would speak to your friends down there
among the Indians and ask for their cooperation. We
don't want any trouble and you may be able to help us
avoid any if you will do as I'm requesting.''

"Neither do I want any trouble, Major, nor do those
people down there want any. So I'll go down and tell
them what's coming down the pike and then the colonel
can give them his orders.''

"Thank you, Mr. Conrad.''

"Stay here,'' Gabe told Sky Walking Woman and
then began to make his way through the camp, advising

its inhabitants that they had been ordered to give any weapons they possessed to the soldiers.

Not one of the men was willing to do so, Gabe soon discovered as the warriors heatedly discussed the order among themselves. "Look," he pleaded with them, "You'll never be able to mount an attack against nearly five hundred men. Not with the few weapons you men say you've got hidden away. To try to make a stand now would only get you all killed. Turn in your weapons and be done with it."

The men ignored him, leaving their tipis to sit on the ground in a semicircle outside them, their women and children remaining inside the tipis by order of Colonel Forsythe.

Gabe, standing behind the seated Indians, watched Lieutenant Kendrick approach and make his announcement.

"All weapons are to be surrendered at once," Kendrick declared in a loud voice. "Twenty men, to be designated by me, will enter their tipis and return with their weapons which they will place on the ground over there." He indicated a spot to the left near where the Indians had left their ponies. Then he stepped forward and, moving among the warriors, tapped twenty of them upon the shoulders.

The twenty men chosen by Kendrick rose and went to their tipis. While they were gone, a thick silence settled over the area. The soft nickering of Gabe's sorrel was the only thing that broke it. When the twenty men returned, they brought with them only two rifles, which they placed near the horses before returning to their places in the group.

They and the soldiers stared stonily at one another.

Finally, Kendrick, nervously slapping a hand against

his thigh, said, "It is perfectly obvious to me that you men are unwilling to obey my order. Two guns? This is laughable. I know you have more than two guns hidden in your tipis or on your persons. I want them *all* surrendered and I want them surrendered *now*!"

No one moved. No one spoke.

An exasperated Kendrick shouted an order to the armed troopers behind him who promptly moved up on foot to within a few yards of the group of seated Indians.

"Search the tipis!" Kendrick ordered another detachment of troopers.

These men stormed the tipis, searching them thoroughly and, in the process, as thoroughly upsetting the women and children as they went about carrying out Kendrick's command.

Gabe watched as buffalo robes used for bedding and cooking utensils were thrown out of some of the tipis by the searchers. He heard the wailing of children and the shrieks of women. His fists clenched at his sides. A muscle in his jaw jumped. His eyes came to rest on the two rifles that had been surrendered.

Minutes passed.

Suddenly, Yellow Bird, the medicine man who had attempted to cure Big Foot of his illness, stood up and began to move among the seated warriors, blowing on an eagle-bone whistle and exhorting the men to rise up and resist the soldiers.

"Do not be afraid, my brothers!" he cried and then blew more shrill notes on his whistle. "Do we not wear our ghost shirts? They make the soldiers powerless and weak. Their bullets cannot harm us. *Resist, my brave brothers!*"

The eerie notes of Yellow Bird's whistle floated

through the camp to blend with the continuing cries of the children and the shrieks of the women coming from inside the tipis. They in turn, blended with the raucous shouts and loud laughter of the still-searching soldiers.

Gabe glanced at Kendrick and then scanned the faces of the troopers. None of them apparently understood the Sioux language, he realized. None of them, at any rate, was showing any reaction to Yellow Bird's militant exhortations.

As Yellow Bird continued his harangue and his now wild whistling, Gabe could see that the medicine man's words were having a definite effect on the warriors. He could see the tensing of their bodies, the narrowing of their eyes, the twitching of their fingers as if they sought the cold iron of a gun's trigger. It's not just Yellow Bird who's got them all on edge, he thought uneasily. It's also the way those troopers are raising Cain among the women and children inside the tipis. They look like they're about ready to explode.

At that moment, the soldiers returned carrying armloads of weapons, a total of nearly forty rifles, which they dumped on the ground beside the other two rifles the Indians had voluntarily surrendered.

Gabe's attention was drawn again to those two weapons, specifically, to the Winchester rifle that looked to him to be serviceable despite the few spots of rust it bore on its barrel. He was wondering if it was loaded, when one of the soldiers, taking Kendrick's search and seizure order very seriously, approached an Indian and lifted the man's blanket.

At that same instant, as women and children flooded out of their tipis, Yellow Bird bent down, scooped up a handful of dust, and tossed it high into the air.

As if Yellow Bird's action had been a signal, one of

the seated men sprang to his feet. Quickly withdrawing a rifle from beneath his blanket, he fired at the soldiers facing him.

Gabe immediately threw himself to the ground, expecting the soldiers to return the unexpected fire, which they promptly did from where they stood, only a few feet away from the Indians. The sound of gunfire thundered in Gabe's ears as he rolled over and then scrambled to his feet. To his right, the ground was littered with bodies, both red and white. Both men and women. And some children.

The warriors who had survived the soldiers' initial onslaught had stripped themselves of their blankets to reveal the revolvers, a few rifles, warclubs, and many knives they had concealed on their bodies.

As Gabe ran toward the Winchester he had had his eye on, the firing became sporadic. Glancing over his shoulder, he saw that the battle had degenerated into vicious hand-to-hand combat, As it was being waged, most of the surviving women and children fled screaming from the camp.

Gabe, as he crouched and picked up the gun he had been after, heard a roaring sound. Turning, he saw the four Hotchkiss guns on the rise open fire on the combatants below them.

They're killing their own men, he thought, unable to believe what he was seeing. And what he was seeing was the slaughter of both soldiers and Indians as the Hotchkiss guns indiscriminately raked the area. He quickly checked the Winchester he had retrieved and found that its chamber held twelve rounds.

Then, nearly blinded by the gunsmoke that was swirling through the camp, he almost failed to see a soldier in the distance raise his rifle and take aim at him. But see him he did, out of the corner of his eye, just in time. Raising the rifle in his hands, he fired a snap shot. The soldier flew backward, dropped his gun, and fell to the ground.

Gabe scanned the area, squinting as he peered through the gunsmoke. He saw no sign of Sky Walking Woman or Warm Blanket. No sign of Hears Thunder, either.

But there were bodies lying everywhere, some of them face down, so it was impossible to tell if any were those of the three people he was searching for. Still crouching, he made his way toward the tipis and turned over the first body he came to.

Yellow Bird. Dead.

He searched among the corpses, seeking but not finding any of the three people he was concerned about. The firing continued but the soldiers who had survived the attack by the Indians and their own unseasoned men had moved away.

Gabe, cautiously raising his head, saw Indians running frantically toward the ravine behind the camp. Soldiers, firing erratically, pursued them, some of them shouting obscenities at the top of their voices.

Gabe saw a woman, a baby in her arms, fall only feet away from the northern bank of the ravine. He rose and ran toward the soldier who had shot the woman as the man took aim at the woman's baby, who had fallen some distance from its mother and now lay waving its arms about and wailing. Bringing his rifle up to his shoulder, he sighted and fired.

His round slammed into the soldier, sending him hurtling forward to fall over the edge of the ravine.

The Hotchkiss guns boomed again, one after the other. Their smoke obliterated the sky. The stench seared Gabe's nostrils as he ran through the camp, turning over bodies, searching for his friends.

The ravine, he thought, when he could not find them in or out of the tipis, alive or wounded or dead. They must have run to the ravine. He headed for it, past tipis which had been set on fire by the Hotchkiss guns as they fired their two-pound artillery shells at the rate of fifty per minute to mow down everything within their lethal range, some of their own soldiers included.

Gabe, as he ran, found himself approaching Big Foot's tipi. As he neared it, he saw the old chief lying dead in front of the shelter on his back, his sightless eyes staring up at a sky he could not see, his body ripped by bullets.

Gabe, his gorge rising, ran on.

As he neared the ravine, he saw a soldier scalping a dead warrior, shouting over and over again as he wielded his knife, *"You bastards killed him. You killed Billy. He was my best friend. You bastards killed him. You killed . . ."*

Gabe passed the grief-crazed soldier and leaped down into the ravine, landing on the bloody body of a slain soldier.

He lost his balance and almost fell. As he struggled to right himself, a soldier leaped down beside him, his face sweating despite the cold December air, and yelled, "They ran west, the sonabitches!" Then he was gone, racing through the ravine in pursuit of his foes.

Gabe raced after him when he heard someone scream in the distance beyond a bend in the ravine. When he rounded that bend, he found no one. He ran on and soon overtook several women and children who were scrambling up the sides of the ravine.

He called out to them, asked them if any of them had

seen Hears Thunder, Sky Walking Woman, or Warm Blanket. At first, they paid no attention to him as they tried to get out of the ravine that had already served as a death trap for so many. He repeated his call for information and this time one of the women pointed mutely to the west.

Then she and the women and children were over the top of the ravine and gone from Gabe's sight.

He ran west.

Within minutes he came upon Hears Thunder. The man was sitting on the ground with his back braced against the southern side of the ravine, his hands folded in front of him, his head bowed as if he were dozing.

Gabe dropped down on one knee beside him and put out a hand. Hears Thunder groaned as Gabe's hand touched his shoulder.

Gabe withdrew his hand as his eyes met those of the man who had become his friend. He stared down at the gaping hole in Hears Thunder's body that the man was trying to cover with his hands. Blood oozed from it. So did slippery white intestines and dark internal organs.

Gut shot.

The words echoed in Gabe's mind. He wanted to help, to do something. But he knew, and it was a terrible knowledge that almost crushed him, that there was nothing he—or anyone—could do for Hears Thunder.

The warrior had begun to whimper. There were tears in his eyes. His lips twisted in agony. His eyes speared Gabe. Asked for help. Asked for the only kind of help that Gabe could give him. Silently asked Gabe to kill him.

Gabe shook his head. He couldn't. He just couldn't.

Hears Thunder moaned again and his eyes continued

to plead with Gabe. His mouth worked but he was past forming words.

Gabe raised his rifle.

Hears Thunder did not flinch. He nodded slightly.

Gabe's finger tightened on his trigger. Loosened. "Sky Walking Woman and Warm Blanket—where?"

Hears Thunder's head turned slightly toward the west. He waited, an odd expression of peace on his face as Gabe's finger again tightened on his trigger.

Gabe fired.

It was over.

He ran on.

He came to a halt when he spotted Warm Blanket lying on the floor of the ravine, two soldiers standing over her, one of them grinning as he buttoned his trousers. A roar of outrage ripped from his throat. He sprang forward, swinging his rifle by the barrel, and bowled both men over. The sound of cracking bone had given him immense satisfaction. He bent down to help Warm Blanket rise.

She shrank from his touch, her eyes wild with fear, an animal that can stand no more torment.

"Warm Blanket," he whispered. "It's Long Rider."

Her eyes were on him but he knew she did not see him. She saw only another man, one who would—

He turned as the light behind him shifted. Just in time. One of the soldiers was on his feet. His rifle was in his hand. Gabe was about to fire in self-defense when Warm Blanket sprang to her feet and darted in front of him, fleeing to the east.

The soldier's shot that had been meant for Gabe caught her high up in the chest and tore through her body, dropping her like a stone.

Gabe fired over her as she fell. His round blew most

of the soldier's head off, spattering the side of the ravine with gray-white brains.

A shot sounded.

Gabe, as the round tore through his left bicep, realized that the other soldier he had downed had regained consciousness. The man was sitting on the ground, his lower jaw broken and hanging open as he levered a round into his rifle's chamber.

Gabe pumped two rounds into the man and then turned and ran.

He ran into Sky Walking Woman, who came wheeling around a bend in the ravine right into his arms. She began to pound his chest with her fists, her eyes squeezed shut, as she screamed senselessly.

"Sky Walking Woman," Gabe said, speaking her name in an effort to calm her as he held her with his left arm which was sending piercing messages of pain to his brain.

If she heard him, she gave no sign. She easily broke free of him and ran back the way he had just come. He heard her cry, *"Aiieee!"*

He knew she had found what she had been looking for—her daughter. He hurried to where she was kneeling and tried to draw her away from the body she was cradling in her arms as she rocked, weeping back and forth.

Suddenly, breaking free of him, she spoke, addressing Warm Blanket's corpse, "Is your uncle with you, my daughter? I have not seen him. When we fled he, tried to fight off the soldiers. He tried to keep them from killing us."

She leaned down as if to hear her daughter's answer.

But it was Gabe who answered her question. "Hears

Thunder is dead, Sky Walking Woman. He died trying to save you both.''

"Aiieee!"

He hunkered down beside her and let her wail. There was nothing he could do. He closed his eyes for a moment, trying to block out the images of death and destruction that surrounded him. When he opened them, he moved swiftly but not swiftly enough.

Sky Walking Woman had seized the sidearm of the dead soldier lying not far away. In one swift movement, she placed its barrel against her left temple and pulled its trigger.

Gabe closed his eyes again. He tried not to see what he suspected he would never be able to forget. But he could still see the corpses of his friends. Hears Thunder. Sky Walking Woman. Warm Blanket, the girl he had helped cross the threshold into womanhood. Dead, all of them.

He threw back his head and howled in pain for a long time. Then, falling silent, he wiped the wetness from his face, rose, and climbed out of the ravine, aware of the blood soaking through the bullet hole in the sleeve of the ghost shirt Sky Walking Woman had given him to protect him from harm.

He walked past a few of the People who were being herded somewhere by soldiers. He walked past the smoking ashes of tipis. He stumbled over a woman's dropped awl case and walked on. When he came to the horses, he moved in among them until he reached his sorrel.

Shoving the rifle he was carrying into his saddle scabbard, he swung aboard the horse and rode out of the camp.

As snow began to fall and he rode on, for one sweet

fleeting moment, he thought they were riding with
him—Warm Blanket, young and lovely; Sky Walking
Woman, with a loving smile on her face for him; and
Hears Thunder, a brave warrior and faithful friend.

But then they were gone.

And he was alone.